Broome Enigma

by

Meryl Brown Tobin

Broome Enigma

Cover Art by *Kristian Norris*

The Wild Rose Press, Inc.
PO Box 708
Adams Basin, NY 14410-0708
Visit us at www.thewildrosepress.com

Publishing History
First Edition, 2023
Trade Paperback ISBN 978-1-5092-5063-9
Digital ISBN 978-1-5092-5064-6

Published in the United States of America

Dedication

To my husband, Hartley Tobin.

Acknowledgments

Thanks to Ally Robertson, The Wild Rose Press editor who valued my work and showed me how to "get over the hump," with the help of freelance editor Tami Jeffers.

A big thank you too, to Val Mathews, The Wild Rose Press editor who earlier steered me in the right direction with advice and recommended the two excellent books, Mary Buckham's *A Writer's Guide to Active Setting* and Janice Hardy's *Understanding Show, Don't Tell*.

A big gust of wind rocked the van and flung Jodie hard against Joe. He pushed her off.

"Joe, it's me, Jodie! Wake up, wake up!"

"Jodie, is that you?" He threw his arms around her and buried his head in her chest.

She brushed his hair back from his sweating face. "Take it easy, Joe. Take deep breaths. It's okay. It's going to be okay."

He stopped shaking and pulled back from her. "What's happening?"

"It's the cyclone. Don't you remember?"

Another huge gust shook the van and sent Jodie sprawling on Joe's bunk and into the wall. "Ow, that hurt!" She picked herself up and rubbed her head.

The van rocked violently again. Joe and Jodie grabbed for handholds.

"Quick, come into my bed with me, Joe. It will be safer there." Tripping and feeling their way along the wall, the two made their way to the double bed and clambered in.

Her breathing coming in short spasms, she lay on her back and took deep breaths. The storm whined and screeched about her, and the roof creaked and scraped. "Oh, my god, the roof's going to take off any minute!"

Joe's arms enveloped her. "Hush, everything will be all right. But will you be okay if we have to make a run for it?"

"Yes." She let out a sob. "But I like our chances better in here than out there."

Joe kissed her forehead. He pulled her closer and they lay locked against each other while the storm raged around them.

Praise for Meryl Brown Tobin

Her work has been shortlisted in competitions run by the Australian Society of Authors Inc., Fellowship of Australian Writers (Victoria), Poetry Matters, Positive Words, Redoubt, The Society of Women Writers Victoria, Waterline Writing Competition, Woman's Day, and Writer's Friend. In 2011 she won The Society of Women Writers, Victoria Inc. Biennial Literary Award for Women for a short story.

Chapter 1

Tiffany gave a fake cough, and Jodie turned and looked up at her sister's flushed face.

Frowning, Jodie lowered the heavy suitcase she'd just lifted out of the boot of her car and placed it on the concrete slab beside her. She glanced around the crowded caravan sites separated by small patches of lawn near their on-site van. Nearby, a young man was bending over sprinklers and moving them about the lawn. Jodie grinned. "Might have known—had to be a guy, didn't it, Tiff?"

As the young man straightened and turned, Jodie whistled soundlessly.

Dressed only in jeans and sandals, the young man with his deep tan and curly brown hair that reached almost to his shoulders glanced over in their direction. Jodie sucked in her breath, and Tiffany gave her a nudge. "Wow-ee, Jodie! He can come around any time."

The older girl pulled a face. "Gee, give him a break. He obviously works here. Let him get on with it." She shoved the suitcase into Tiff's hands and steered her toward their van.

"How do you like that tan? And that dark hair? And those muscles? Bet he's got big brown eyes you could drown in."

"Stop drooling."

1

"But what a spunk. It's like having Tom Cruise around."

"Who's Tom Cruise?"

"Jodie, it is 1986. What rock have you been living under? Tom Cruise's a film star—you know, the one in *Top Gun*."

"Oh, him. Yeah, maybe your spunky guy does look a bit like him, but his hair's curlier." From the van window, she studied him walking across the lawn.

Joining her, Tiffany gave her another nudge. "Isn't he a hunk?"

Her heart fluttering, Jodie nodded. "Not bad. Even his five o'clock shadow looks good." She turned to Tiffany. "But don't get any ideas about him, little sister—you're only here a week, remember?"

"So-ooo—plenty can happen in a week."

"He's too old for you."

"I'm eighteen…"

Jodie sighed.

Tiff sniffed and jerked her shoulder. "He can't be more than twenty-four or twenty-five."

As Jodie swept her hand through her blond cropped hair and cooling air reached her scalp, she smiled. *I wonder if he's too old for a twenty-two-year-old. No, just right.* A shiver rippled through her.

Jodie returned to her small green hatchback and started to take out a second load of gear. Footsteps approached. The hair on the back of her neck prickled. Assuming a disinterested expression, she glanced around at Tiffany who was standing on their caravan step and running her hand down her long russet hair. The young man walked past and she flipped it back in a flirtatious manner. "Hi."

Unsmiling, he nodded and continued to walk toward the tent beside their van.

Jodie groaned. *Bet he reckons, not another bimbo—sure to be an occupational hazard for him here.* He glanced back and took a look at Jodie. Her nails dug into her palms.

She stared at the closing tent flap. *Hey, Tom Cruise, you don't need to snub our Goldie Hawn. Tiff's not that bad when you get to know her.*

Tiffany gave a big grin and winked at Jodie.

Jodie glared. "Don't you dare see him as a challenge." With a sigh, she reached into the boot of her car and pulled out her painting equipment.

Tiffany clapped her hands. "Did you see the Spunk go into the tent next door? He must be our next-door neighbor—yippee!"

Jodie pushed her easel into Tiffany's hands. In an exaggerated show of losing her balance Tiffany fell backwards and then regained her feet. "Hey, are we going sightseeing before you settle down to painting or what?"

"Going sightseeing, of course. I want to see the place as much as you do. How can I do my series of Broome paintings if I don't get to see Broome first?"

Her sister pouted. "Don't expect me to lie on the ground beside your easel while you paint masterpieces for Kenny."

"This week's purely exploratory. Mainly photos, I promise."

"Cool." Tiffany unpacked the car fridge she had carried in. "Make sure you get the Spunk next door in the photos though."

"Fine. Just stow him under the bonnet or

something."

"I'll do better than that. Once I get to talk to him, I'll ask him along. Then he and I can sit in the back while you play chauffeur."

A sponge flew across the room and landed in Tiffany's lap. "Stop being impossible and wipe down the table."

Tiffany turned on the tap. "What sort of a place is this? There's no water. I'll check the hose." From outside, she called, "The hose is connected. Give me a tick and I'll follow it to wherever the tap is."

She returned with a frown.

"What now?"

"There's a set of six taps in the middle of the lawn but they've all got hoses attached. Our hose is lying on the ground under the tap attached to the sprinklers."

Jodie feigned a deadpan expression. "Better have a word with the Spunk then."

"Why didn't I think of that myself?"

The young man next door emerged from his tent and walked over to the sprinklers and moved them along. Tiffany raced out after him. "Excuse me, do you work here?" She opened up her arms to encompass the whole caravan park.

The young man looked up at the neat figure in her brief top and short shorts who was giving him a smile brilliant enough to dazzle a rock star.

"I do a bit of gardening and maintenance about the park. Something wrong?"

Tiffany pouted. "Yes—we've got no water in our on-site van."

"Sorry, there aren't enough taps to go around, so I have to take them where and when I can find them."

Like a pretty little girl, Tiff wrinkled her brow.

"When a caravan moved off next to your site this morning, I had to water the grass. Your van was vacant at the time, so I took your hose off the tap it was on."

Tiffany fluttered her eyelashes. "But there are only six taps and there are hoses on all of them."

"That's right."

"Well, where are the taps for the caravanners who don't currently have hoses or who have hoses that aren't connected?"

The man gave a self-deprecating smile. "They're the only taps in this part of the park, apart from the ones over the trough in the laundry and one outside the laundry."

"Great. Jodie will be thrilled."

"Jodie?"

"My sister." She pointed to the van, and Jodie quickly stepped out of sight behind a curtain. "Me, I'm Tiffany, Tiff for short. And you're...?"

"Um, Joe." He swallowed. "Look, I'm sorry about your not having any water."

"That's okay. When do we get it back?"

As Joe took one of the hoses off one of the taps, Jodie sighed and shook her head in mock disbelief. *Boy, Tiff, I don't know what you said then, but you sure know how to get guys to do what you want. Wish you'd share the power with me.*

Moments later the sprinklers went off. Jodie exhaled audibly. *At least I can wipe down the table now.*

As Tiffany stepped into the van, Jodie looked up. "Did you find out The Spunk's name and whatever?"

"I thought you weren't interested."

"I'm not, but if he's a neighbor, we can't go around calling him The Spunk."

"It's Joe, and he wasn't a tiny bit cool about having to make excuses for his boss."

"Don't blame Joe then. Here we are in an idyllic location laid out with tropical palms, and it looks as if his boss keeps piling in the vans and tents. There seem to be two or three on every site. No wonder there aren't enough taps to go around."

Tiffany's eyes glazed over. "Wonder how Joe came to be working here. With those looks, you'd think he'd be on the telly or something."

After the sisters showered in the small amenities block nearby, Jodie snuggled down into the double bed at the back of the van. Tiffany clambered into one of the single bunks nearer the front and placed her arms under her head. "While I'm here, I'm going to have a great time with Joe. I can feel it."

Jodie pulled her pillow over her head. *Not if I can help it. If I'm lucky, maybe he and I might find we've got something in common.* Soon she fell asleep dreaming she and Joe swam about like dolphins in the ocean.

Distant yells and thumps woke her from a deep sleep.

A note of fear in her voice, Tiffany called softly, "Are you awake, Jodie? What do you reckon is going on?"

"No idea. But it doesn't sound too near us so I'm not going out to investigate." Eyes shut tight, she was soon breathing rhythmically again. *Wait for me, Joe.*

****

A basket of dirty washing on her hip, Jodie made

her way to the laundry. The flap of the tent next door opened, and Joe emerged. The sleeves of his long-sleeved blue shirt were rolled up to the elbow. Casually buttoned with only three or four buttons, the shirt opened at the top revealing tanned chest. Goose bumps flared on Jodie's arms.

As he came closer, a blush stained her cheeks. "Hear the disturbance in the night, Joe?" His name caught in her throat and she squirmed.

"Yes. A group of hoons came in and smashed up the boom gate out the front."

"Why?"

"Too much drink."

"Delightful." *Tiff's right—this is the place for adventures, even if some are not very nice ones.* She smiled at Joe and he nodded and she continued walking to the laundry.

With the washing churning around in the washing machine, Jodie rejoined Tiffany for breakfast. "All the line space outside the small amenities block is gone already, Tiff. Maybe we should see if we can get our money back and find somewhere less crowded."

"No way. Give it a week."

Jodie gave a crooked smile. "Until you've gone home, you mean."

The younger girl jumped up. "Hey, there's Joe."

Goose bumps flared on Jodie's arms again.

Tiffany stared out the window. "Why do you think he looks so...so pre-occupied? How can someone so handsome not seem to realize it? It's as if he's wrapped in a cocoon. I wish he'd smile a bit more too—he hardly ever smiles, and when he does it just about blinds you."

"Stop romanticizing. Next you'll be telling me he's The Sleeping Spunk and you're the beautiful princess whose kiss will bring him back to life."

"What a good idea. I'll go and try it now, eh?"

Jodie grabbed her before she got to the door.

****

At the laundry, Tiffany gave Jodie a wave. "While you get the washing out of the washing machine, I'll see if there's any line space on one of the lines near the big amenities block we checked out last night."

Joe walked past the laundry and glanced in.

Jodie straightened up. "Oh, Joe, is that full clothesline just there the only line for people in this part of the park?"

His deep brown eyes with their sweeping black lashes held her gaze. She gulped.

"Yes, but there are other lines near the main amenities block you can use."

"I know but that's a long way to carry a basket of wet clothes. Aren't there any closer?"

He shook his head, and Jodie rolled her eyes. "I'm sorry, I'm not having a go at you. It's just my boss told me this place was fantastic, so I was expecting more." *Stop babbling, Jodie.* "The overcrowding's terrible—you wouldn't want there to be a fire."

"It's been worse."

"You're joking."

"No. Gilbert, the owner, hates turning anyone away."

"Don't others complain?"

Joe shrugged. "I wouldn't know. But if anyone complains to me, I pass on their complaints."

The edges of his mouth turned up a fraction, and

Jodie's heart did a flip.

Joe smiled. "How about I carry your washing to the line for you?"

"Th-thanks." As he bent down to pick up the washing basket, his face came close to Jodie's legs, and they buckled.

Beside a vacant space on the partly-filled line outside the main amenities block, Tiffany stood sentinel. At the approach of Jodie with Joe, her mouth fell open.

As Joe placed the basket at her feet, she stepped back. "Hi, Joe. Thanks for that. Trust Jodie to have you working."

Jodie converted a laugh into a cough.

"Part of the service. Enjoy your stay in Broome." With a salute, he walked off.

Tiffany gave her brow an elaborate wipe. "What a spunky hunk!"

Tingles shot in all directions throughout Jodie's body. Her back to her sister, she started to peg out clothes.

Tiffany shot her a questioning look. "How did you get him to carry the washing basket?"

"I had a whinge about the management of the park."

"You didn't."

"Sure did."

"Gee, we'll be lucky if he ever talks to us again."

A smile on her face, Jodie continued to peg out the washing.

Chapter 2

A man on a bike rode towards the girls standing outside their van. Eyes brightening as he approached, Tiffany stepped forward. "Hi, Joe, off to the shops?"

"Yes."

"Like to come in the car with us then?"

Jodie's mouth dropped open.

"We'll be going in a few minutes, won't we, Jodie?"

Before she could answer, Joe rode on. "No, thanks."

Tiffany watched him weave around some vans. "Well, that takes the cake!"

Her sister slid into the driver's seat of her car. "You mean *you* take the cake."

"I was just being neighborly."

"Pull the other one."

Tiffany shrugged one shoulder. "You know this guy's starting to get me with his Greta Garbo act—one minute he's come hither eye-balling, the next standing-off."

"He's what?"

"You heard. It's also a mystery that, though he's living like a back-packer, he doesn't seem to be one."

At the entrance to the park, a workman was mending the broken boom gate. Jodie slowed down almost to a stop. The man looked up and waved her through.

Along the other side of the road, cars and vans were lined up. Jodie frowned. "Broome must be hard up for caravan parks if they queue this early in the morning for this one. Hey, is that a cyclist I can see in the distance?"

Leaning forward, Tiffany peered into the distance. "No." She slumped back in her seat.

Jodie took deep breaths. "Easy to get addicted to this, eh?"

With a casual wave of her hand, Tiffany straightened up and embraced the scenery. "What—the blue skies, the warm sun, the swaying palms, and the clean balmy breezes?"

"You got it." Around a corner, Jodie's heart lifted. "Hey, there's Joe!"

Her head out the window, Tiffany waved like a cheerleader as they passed him. He continued to pedal steadily.

Jodie glanced at her sister. "Did he wave back?"

Tiffany's expression drooped. "Sort of—he nodded."

"Perhaps he prefers a more subtle approach."

Her lower lip jutting out, Tiffany crossed her arms across her chest. "Like what?"

"More low key maybe."

Tiffany shrugged.

"Come on, Tiff, time to lose the sulks or you'll miss Chinatown."

"Chinatown? That's the old part of Broome, isn't it?" She leaned forward. "Can we stop off at the jetty to see that eight-meter rise and fall of the tide they rave about?"

"Okay, we'll stop at Streeter's Jetty—that's where the luggers come in at high tide."

Very old buildings stood along Carnarvon Street. Jodie grinned. "Reckon a camel train could do a U-turn in this street in the old days?"

"Is that why it's so long and wide?"

"So the tourist literature says."

Her eyes shining, Tiffany pointed to a big old corrugated-tin building with a double gable roof. "See that Sun Pictures sign on the roof? That must be Broome's famous open-air picture theater. Can we pull up to have a better look?" She grinned. "Besides, that'll give Joe a sporting chance to catch up."

"You're incorrigible."

As they toured Chinatown on foot, Jodie stared at some of the older buildings. "Wow, I can't wait to turn these into paintings. These shops must be standing much as they would have stood a century ago—except for their obvious aging and relative lack of maintenance, of course." She took out her camera.

"No, you can do that later. Time to see what's inside these shops now." Grabbing her hand, Tiffany dragged Jodie into an old shop. A woman storekeeper of Chinese appearance smiled and nodded to them. Tiffany smiled back. "Hello. Is it okay if we look around?"

Again, the storekeeper smiled and nodded. This time she also gestured with her hand for them to wander around.

Stopping at a display stand, Tiffany pointed to a yellow tee shirt with a red and green painted dragon shooting forth red flames. "Think I'd impress Joe if I wore that?"

"Who knows, but it would look good on you." Jodie picked up a black tee shirt with a red pearling lugger on it. "How about this one for me?" She held it up against her chest. *I wonder if Joe would like it.* She snatched it down. *Don't be so stupid—I couldn't care less what he thinks.* She handed it to the store-keeper who smiled, nodded, and wrapped it up.

Jodie took the parcel from her. "Thank you. Your tee shirts are lovely. You must sell lots of them."

The woman said something in Chinese, clasped her hands together, and bowed.

Jodie smiled and bowed back. *It's like being in another world.*

As the sisters walked along the jetty on the edge of Roebuck Bay, Tiffany pointed to several pearl luggers coming in. "Guess they're coming in to unload their catch and refuel."

Jodie took a photo of a dark green lugger standing straight and tall. "Beauty. Now, if we come back at low tide, I should get a matching shot of it stranded in mud."

At the packing shed at the end of the jetty, sorters sorted the pearl shell into different piles. Tiffany's eyes widened. "Gee, how can their hands move that fast?"

Jodie looked around the old shed "You could get very history-minded in a place like this. It's like walking into a past era."

Back at the car she flipped through travel literature. "Want a two-minute history lesson?"

Tiffany groaned.

"The Aborigines were here first—maybe for 40,000 years. Then they reckon the Malays probably stopped off here to collect pearls and hunt for turtles and dugongs. The Dutch came next—in 1644 when Abel Tasman sailed in close to shore. Then the English buccaneer William Dampier landed here in 1699. After Captain Cook's voyage in 1770, Great Britain claimed the whole country…"

"Your two minutes is up."

Jodie jabbed at a page. "Then Phillip Parker King, sailed along the coast in 1819. John and Alexander Forrest came along in the 1870s and pastoralists followed in the early 1880s. There."

"What about the pearlers?"

"Hmm, looks like they came about the same time as the pastoralists. This booklet says Broome was established in 1883—after they discovered pearling grounds off the coast. They also traded in tortoise shell. By 1900, four hundred luggers were based here. How's that?"

Tiffany looked up and grabbed Jodie's arm. "Isn't that Joe?"

Jodie's head jerked around. A middle-aged man was riding a bike toward them.

"Gotcha!"

Both girls giggled.

At the Pioneer Cemetery near Town Beach the girls walked around the lawns and among graves. Beside an old grave, Tiffany paused and peered at the inscription. "This one's dated 1880. I reckon it could be the oldest grave here."

As she walked toward the beach, Jodie stared out to sea. "At low tide, they say you can pick out the remains of three of the sixteen flying boats sunk by Japanese warplanes on the third of March, 1942."

Shielding her eyes with her hand, Tiffany looked

out to sea too. "Doesn't sound good."

"No." Jodie consulted a book in her hand. "Broome and its port weren't even defended then. Japanese warplanes just flew in and shot down an airplane carrying wounded people that had taken off for Perth. Then they destroyed fifteen of the Dornier flying boats anchored in the bay. These boats were filled with refugees, mostly women and children. Many of them were killed outright or as they swam through burning oil that had ignited during the attack. When the Japanese got to the airfield, they destroyed lots of planes there as well. Altogether, they killed seventy people and wiped out twenty-four aircraft."

Tiffany shook her head. "Was that worse than the raid over Darwin in 1942?"

"No, Darwin copped the worst air raid in Australia's history, and Broome the second-worst."

"It mustn't have been much fun living here during the war." Her shoulders hunched over, Tiffany turned and headed back toward the car. "Come on, let's go. This place depresses me. Let's find Joe instead."

Her face tightening, Jodie ran and fell into step beside her. "How about we slowly drive up and down the streets of Broome? Whenever we see something interesting, we can pull up and get out and walk."

"Fine by me as long as the something interesting is Joe."

"Cut it out, Tiff. You're so obvious, it isn't funny."

Near the post office stood an old colonial building with wide verandas on stilts. Tiffany looked at a sign. "It's the courthouse."

Jodie took a photo of it. "Wow, I'd love a piece of charcoal handy so I could start sketching it."

The Japanese and Chinese cemeteries were situated side by side. As she and Tiffany wandered among the unusual headstones made from local sandstone rocks, Jodie stopped and peered at a sign. Tiffany groaned. "Another history lesson."

"Not getting bored, are we?"

"If you hadn't given Joe the frozen fish-face treatment, he could have taken us around. I wouldn't be bored then."

"I'll keep it in mind for next time, okay?"

"Promise?"

"Yes. Now please read the sign and tell me about this column while I take a photo of it."

"It's a memorial to forty Japanese seamen lost in the 1908 cyclone." Tiffany shuddered. "Altogether one hundred and fifty seamen were lost."

A nearby monument with a steel diving helmet celebrated the centenary of Japanese involvement in the pearling industry. Tiffany rubbed her nose. "I wonder if Joe's a diver in his spare time. He can't just be the hired help at the caravan park."

Someone cycled up behind them, and the girls looked around. Tiffany started to run her hand down her long hair as the male cyclist stopped and got off the bike. She flicked her hair back. "Hi, Joe. I must be magic. I mention you and there you are—like a genie popping out of a bottle."

Cool it, Tiff. Can't you see Joe's having trouble keeping a straight face? She smiled at him and he smiled back. Pleasurable little shivers ran down her spine.

With an extra flick of her hair, Tiffany stepped toward him. "What are you doing here?"

Jodie glared.

"I come here for a break from the caravan park. It's a place full of history, and I like that."

Tiffany raised her eyebrows. "Some of it is pretty grim."

"Yeah, I know. Did you guys know Broome was virtually a military garrison in World War II?"

"No, but we've just read the Japanese raided it."

"That's because the airfield was a base for refueling planes from the Philippines and Indonesia. They were flying out wounded soldiers and civilians before the Japanese got to those countries."

Jodie gave a silent whistle. "Scary times. What happened to the Japanese divers and crewmen who lived here? Were they treated as aliens?"

"Yes. There were five hundred of them, and they all had to be interned."

"What happened to the rest of the people in Broome?"

"They evacuated the women and children."

Tiffany ran her hand over a headstone. "Sounds awful. We're lucky we're here now and not then. Would you like to take us around the rest of the town and tell us more about it?"

"Another time perhaps." Joe hopped on his bike and rode off.

Tiffany pouted.

An attractive brown-skinned woman with two curly-haired children walked past.

When she was twenty meters past, Tiffany shook her head. "Wow, what a stunning-looking lady. What do you reckon her background is?"

"Who knows? Something exotic—maybe a mix of

Aborigine, Japanese, Chinese, and maybe Malay. Could even be some Filipina and Koepanger."

"Co-what?"

"Koepanger—from East Indonesia."

"Perhaps that's why Joe's so dark—maybe he's got some of whatever you said in him."

****

At the supermarket checkout, Tiffany clutched Jodie's arm. "Hey, isn't that Joe?"

Sighing, Jodie turned and looked at the young man paying for his purchases several checkouts up. Butterflies started to fly up and down inside her stomach.

In the car park, the girls walked near Joe, who was strapping a carton onto the back of his bike. Jodie stopped beside him. "Hi."

As though she hadn't seen him, Tiffany continued on with her trolley.

Jodie stifled a laugh. "Like us to take your shopping back to camp for you? Payment for your lumping our clothes basket."

"Thanks."

He went up to Tiffany, who was unpacking her trolley. She glanced at him. "Hello, fancy catching up with you again."

Unsmiling, he nodded.

Jodie frowned. *What's with you? Does it cost you something to smile? Old Tiff's not that bad and she is trying not to come on so strong.*

Joe turned to Jodie. "Where would you like me to put my groceries?"

****

As Jodie drove through Broome, Tiffany touched

her arm. "How about we go back to the caravan park via Streeter's Jetty to see how the luggers are getting on?"

They walked along the jetty and Tiffany stared at the luggers. "Poor things, stuck in mud, they're nothing like the tall, majestic vessels they were earlier today."

Jodie stopped. "Do you reckon this is the spot where I took my photo this morning?" She sized up a shot. "These luggers will look stunning on canvas."

Almost back to camp, Jodie passed Joe, but he had his head down and made no sign he saw her and Tiffany. Jodie glanced at her sister. "C'mon, aren't you going to throw your head out the window and call out to him?"

She shook her head.

"What, the big love affair gone cold?"

"Don't be silly. It's obvious, isn't it?"

"What is?"

"Joe isn't into exuberant young women—he wants someone more sophisticated."

"Oh."

"I'll let him make the approaches in his own time—you can't rush a deep guy like that."

"He's deep now, is he?"

"Stop laughing at me. You know what I mean."

"What, that Joe's a very private guy for whatever reason and that he's not interested in a flirtation with a girl who'll be around for only a few days?"

"He's not to know that. Anyway, it's a week, and, as I told you before, a lot can happen in a week."

Jodie smiled. *Now that's a thought.*

A long line of vehicles, many of them towing vans, queued up on the road to the park. Glowering, Tiffany threw up her hands. "Oh, no, how are we going to get in?"

"Take our turn, I guess."

Ten minutes later Jodie turned into the caravan park entrance. A bicycle followed her on the inside.

"Joe!" Tiffany started to wave madly and then stopped. "Uh, oh, gently, gently, catchee handsome spunkee."

"How's that, Tiff, Joe riding on our inside past the queue of cars and around the corner toward his camp? Now we know why he prefers a bike—it's quicker."

Another ten minutes later, Jodie got to Gilbert, waiting on his motorbike to take a new caravaner to his van site. She nodded to him. "Another traffic jam?"

His toothpaste-ad smile dropped a little.

As Jodie drove on, Tiffany smacked her lightly on the arm. "Don't be cruel. Think of all the dollars he's making."

At their van, Jodie pulled up and started to unload.

Joe appeared behind her. "Okay if I get my shopping?"

Her knees buckling, Jodie reached into the boot for his box of groceries while Tiffany disappeared into the van.

When Jodie carried in their shopping, Tiffany looked up from the magazine she was reading. "Did he ask you about me?"

"Who?"

Tiffany glared. "Joe, of course."

"No."

"What did he say then?"

"Nothing."

"He must have said something."

"How about 'Thanks'?"

"I give up."

"Maybe you should."

"Oh, you!"

Ignoring her, Jodie got them both a drink of orange juice. While she sipped hers, she looked out the window. A smile crept across her face and she glanced at her watch. "I think we'd better get in the washing. Want to come?"

"All right, anything to get out of this dump for a bit."

On the way to the line, Tiffany drew in her breath. "Hey, do you see what I see?"

Her face as innocent as a toddler's, Jodie looked in the same direction as Tiff. "What?"

"Those four guys at the old microbus—they must belong to the hiking tents pitched near it."

As Tiffany and Jodie walked past the young men, the men winked at each other. The red-haired one called, "Hi."

When they were well past, Tiffany punched the sky. "Wow, wow, wow!"

On their return the young men were still talking outside their microbus. The red-haired one waved. "Hi, again. Been here long?"

Tiffany flicked her hair back and fluttered her long lashes up and down. "Since yesterday." She stayed to talk and Jodie continued to their van with the washing.

At Joe's tent she glanced in. *Blow, no sign of him… Stop feeling so let down. Who cares?*

Half an hour later, eyes shining, Tiffany burst in to the van. "Guess what. Ryan, Pete, Trent, and Wacko are going to the open-air picture theater tonight. They said we can go with them if we like. What do you say?"

"No."

"What do you mean? It'll be cool. The guys are great. Pete's the nice one with the flattop haircut, Ryan's the redhead, Trent's got the lazy smile, and Wacko's the comedian."

Jodie added lines to the palm tree she was sketching.

"Are you listening to me, Jodie?"

"Of course."

"Well, are you going or not?"

"I said no. I don't know them from Adam."

"But I do. I'll introduce you."

With a roll of her eyes, Jodie gripped her pencil hard and drew bold lines on her sketch.

"Gee, you used to be fun—now you're such a spoil-sport. I've a good mind to go without you." Tiffany flounced off, grabbed a magazine, and went to lie on her bunk.

Jodie sighed. *How can I survive another five days of this?* She glanced outside the van window. Her next-door neighbor was walking past. Her body tingled again. *How can I survive another five days and more of this?*

Chapter 3

Most of the seats in the open-air theater were full, and many of the occupants had brought blankets. Jodie glanced around at the people around her in heavy jackets and beanies. "Maybe we should have put on warmer clothes."

Busy whispering to the red-headed Ryan on her far side, Tiffany made no response.

Staring at the film, Joe sat on Jodie's left. She glanced down. *I'd like to enjoy the show too, but someone's long leg is only centimeters from mine, and it's putting me off.* As if belonging to a dangling marionette, her feet shuffled.

At the end of the film, Tiffany stood up and started to follow Ryan and his friends out of the theatre. Jodie tugged at her sleeve. "Where are you off to?"

"Ryan wants me to go home in the microbus with him and his friends. Okay with you?"

"You know the deal."

"Please."

Jodie shrugged her shoulders resignedly. "Just a minute." She turned and whispered to Joe and then turned back to Tiffany. "Tell Ryan he can come with us if he likes."

Quickly Tiffany spoke to him. He grinned and gave a message to Trent who relayed it down the line to the other two young men. Her face glowing, Tiffany grabbed the car keys and, hand in hand with Ryan, hurried out to Jodie's car.

The other boys called, "See ya," and headed off.

Jodie whispered to Joe, "Looks like you've scored the front seat."

With a look of baby innocence on her face, Tiffany clipped on her seatbelt. "Okay if the boys come in for supper? Ryan's already said he'd like to come, haven't you, Ryan?" She bestowed a dazzling smile on him.

Jodie took several deep breaths. *Why am I always placed in the role of the party-pooping big sister? After all, Tiff is eighteen, even if she does behave like a sixteen-year-old at times. Why did Dad put the hard word on me to be responsible for both of us?* "Sorry, Tiff, it's a bit late."

Tiffany pulled a face and Ryan squeezed her hand. "No sweat—we'll get up early tomorrow and take it from there."

Back at the caravan, Tiffany said goodbye to Ryan. He headed off and she went into the van. Standing outside beside Jodie, Joe looked into her eyes. "Thanks for the lift. See you."

Jodie smiled and went into the van. *Be still, insides*

As the sisters undressed for bed, Tiffany had a puzzled look on her face. "You never told me how you got Joe to chaperon us at the pictures with the boys. How did you do it?"

"Maybe he's fallen madly in love with you and couldn't bear the thought of your being alone with four other guys?"

"Then he's left it a bit late to make his run. Tomorrow Ryan and I will be an item on Cable Beach."

A warm feeling enveloped Jodie. *Great, we're no*

longer in competition for the same guy. "Hey, hang on. You didn't ask me if he could come with us to Cable Beach tomorrow."

"That's because I knew what you'd say."

Jodie frowned. *What sort of a sister am I? Tiff must think I'm over-protective and always on guard for both of us.*

"The guys are spending most of the day at the beach so I told Ryan I'd meet him there."

"Gee, I'm going to have a great day, aren't I?"

"You've got the choice of the other guys, and there's always Joe if you go for an older man."

"What do you mean? Joe's not coming."

"Well, I invited him and he didn't say no."

Taking a deep breath, Jodie lay down. Confusing thoughts and strange feelings pulsated through her. *It's like when I sat next to Joe. Why did he come to the pictures with us in the first place? Was it really as he'd said—that he'd never been to the open-air picture theater before and this was a chance to go?* She turned her pillow over and punched it. *No, it's because he'd read my concern to do the right thing, whatever that was, by my scatty but legally adult kid sister.*

She smiled. *You made a great chaperon, Joe— thank you.* She rolled over and hugged her pillow tight.

****

Outside Joe's tent, Jodie gave a cough. "Are you up yet, Joe?"

As he threw open the tent flap, she got a glimpse of his half-eaten breakfast on a heavy wooden table. *That's a strange piece of furniture for a tent.*

"Hi, Jodie. Everything okay?"

"Sort of. Tiff's arranged to meet the boys at Cable

Beach today." She reddened. "Y-you w-wouldn't like to spend the day with us, w-would you? We can leave after you've done your morning jobs for Gilbert and get back in time for your afternoon ones."

He looked closely at her. "Fine, Tiffany did mention it, thanks. I'll be free at nine-thirty. Give me a call when you're ready."

Wow, how easy was that.

When she told Tiffany the news, Tiffany jumped out of bed and hugged her. "I hereby bequeath any interest I might have had in Mr. Joe Mysterious Stranger Spunk to my big sister, Jodie."

Inside, her big sister tingled. "Don't be silly."

****

From the back seat, Joe leaned forward. "Like to see a few of the sights on the drive to Cable Beach?"

Jodie nodded, but Tiffany's mouth tightened into a straight line.

Joe raised his eyebrows. "If you want to see the deepwater port for big boats, we could drive via Broome Jetty at Deep Water Point."

At the jetty, they stood for several minutes looking at the red cliffs and turquoise water. Her camera poised, Jodie stared through its lens. "Magic."

Tiffany jumped from foot to foot. "Come on, at this rate we'll never get to Cable Beach."

Along the jetty, several of the many people fishing showed the group their catches. Against his chest, a man held a gigantic reddish-orange circular fish. Photographers clicked away. Jodie put her camera back in its camera case. "Joe, do you know what that fish is called?"

"A moonfish."

Farther along, Tiffany pointed to another fish. "What's that smaller, silvery one?"

The man who caught it turned to her. "A trevally, love. Like it? If you want one or any other deepwater fish, come here at the change of tide and try your luck." He gave her a wink. "You'll have to build your muscles up first though. It takes a lot to land a beauty like this one."

As the group walked on, Tiffany turned to Joe. "How come you can catch the big deepwater fish here and don't need to go out in a boat?"

"Because of the tide's huge eight-meter rise and fall. In spring it's even better because the tide varies even more—there's eleven meters between high and low tide."

Jodie let out a low whistle. "Wow, Joe, that's the closest you've ever come to making a speech."

He grinned, and the skin crinkled around his eyes.

Tiffany hit her toe on a plank sticking up on the floor of the jetty. "Gee, that hurt, and we've still got a long way to go. How long's this jetty, Joe? A kilometer?"

"Nearly. More than 800 meters, anyway."

At the end of the jetty, people stood watching a large cargo boat being loaded with frozen prawns. Boxes of them were placed in ropes, raised high, and deposited in the boat's hold. Tiffany turned and started to head back. Jodie glanced at Joe. "I wish we could take our time and not have to rush for Tiff."

With a wink, Joe grabbed her hand to hurry her along after Tiffany, whose hair streamed after her as she strode along the jetty. Tingles shot up Jodie's hand and arm.

Along the road to Cable Beach, Jodie turned off onto a corrugated road. Tiffany glared at her. "Hey, what are you driving down here for? This isn't the road to Cable Beach."

"No, but it's taking us to Riddell Beach. Remember, Joe is showing us the sights en route, and this is one of them."

As they stood looking at spectacular rich red cliffs running down to a much lighter-colored rocky platform and narrow sandy beach and turquoise sea, Jodie shook herself. "It doesn't look real, does it?"

Tiffany snorted. "No, so let's get moving." She raced ahead.

Jodie raised her eyebrows. "Sisters, who needs them?" She turned back to the landscape and seascape before them. "I can't wait to paint these cliffs." She raised her camera and took a photo.

"You're an artist?"

"Sort of. I'm taking a holiday from my regular job so I can produce a book of paintings on Broome."

"Are you doing it on spec?"

"No, my boss is a publisher and it was his idea. Until he sees some of my completed paintings though, he can't make a definite commitment."

Joe nodded.

Jodie colored. *I hope he doesn't think I'm big-noting myself.*

At Gantheaume Point, the three young people gazed at spectacular sandstone outcrops in orange, rust, and pink hues and then scrambled over them to the point. Jodie stopped and looked around. "This place must be really something at sunrise and sunset, Joe."

"Yes, the rocks glow, and they've been doing it for

a hundred and ten million years."

Jodie laughed. "You're good at this, you know. Have you ever thought of being a tour guide?"

He shook his head.

Jodie sighed. *A screen's come down over your eyes again. Why can't I mention your past without your blocking me out?*

Tiffany pouted. "Come on, didn't you say we have to see some dinosaur footprints as well?"

Joe pointed out to sea. "Yes, about thirty meters out, but you can only see them at a low king tide. Come and I'll show you a cement cast of them. Don't expect it to be a hundred and thirty million years old though."

Laughing, Jodie jumped across the rocks after him. When Tiffany joined them, she held up her camera. "Stay like that." She snapped a photo of them beside the cast.

Abruptly Joe turned away. "Not me, I'm photo-shy."

"Too late."

Jodie frowned. *Oh, oh, there's no way he wants a photo taken of himself.* A sharp hurt shot through her.

Joe glared. "Then delete it, thanks."

Tiffany pulled a face. Jodie looked hard at Joe. *Geez, someone's acting out of character.*

Glancing at Tiffany's mutinous face, he added, "Come on, I'll show you Anastasia's Pool on the north side of the point." He grabbed Jodie's hand to help her over some big rocks. A tingle shot up her arm.

Situated on a rocky platform high above the sea, the rock pool was full of water. Jodie smiled. "Gee, that's inviting. How did this come to be here?"

"One story reckons a pearler had the pool made as

a safe swimming place for his wife. Another story says a lighthouse keeper built it for his wife who couldn't walk."

Tiffany gave a sniff. "Lucky Anastasia."

****

At Cable Beach, Tiffany threw open the car door and raced up to the top of a dune. Opening her arms, she embraced the kilometers of white sands lapped by a low surf and stretching as if endlessly to her left and for some distance to her right.

Joe and Jodie came up and stood beside her. Jodie sucked in her breath. "Do you know how the beach got its name, Joe?"

"Because of the cable reaching from here across the Timor Sea to Java. The courthouse you saw yesterday used to be Cable House where they kept the transmitting equipment."

Tiffany waved madly. "Ryan!" She flew down the lawn sloping onto the beach. Behind her at a slower pace, the others followed. Joe carried Jodie's sun umbrella and car fridge. He set up the umbrella a discreet distance from the pile of gear dumped on the sand beside Ryan and his friends.

Jodie sighed. "Sometimes I feel more like Tiff's mother than her sister. Have you got any sisters, Joe?"

His face tightened and he turned away.

Frowning, Jodie stared out to sea. Stripped down to her high-cut one-piece aqua swimsuit, Tiffany was splashing around on the water's edge with Ryan and his friends.

Glancing at Joe, Jodie threw her hat down on her towel. "Looks lovely out there. Feel like going in yet?"

Nodding, Joe unzipped his jeans.

Quickly Jodie looked away. *Don't you dare think those thoughts.* With her back to Joe, she pulled off her shorts and tee shirt. Dressed in a royal-blue swimsuit covered in hibiscus flowers, a swimsuit with a cut more modest than her sister's, she followed Joe down to the water. *Thank goodness I'm behind you and can study you and not vice versa. Tiff's right—you are some sexy spunk even if you don't seem aware of it.*

Swimming about in the cool water, Jodie closed her eyes. *Must be how a dolphin feels in its watery heaven.* From time to time she glanced at the tanned and muscular young man diving and swimming around with her. As he performed another swim stroke, their eyes met. "Very impressive."

He gave a wide grin.

A tennis ball splashed in the water near Jodie, and she swam and retrieved it. Treading water and arm raised high, she looked about. A young man's voice called her name. Smiling, she hurled the ball as hard as she could to Ryan who was standing in shallow water beside Tiffany.

Side by side, Jodie and Joe left the water. Her hand ached. *Why don't you hold my hand, you big clunk?*

Toweling herself down, she turned away from him. "I guess I'd better put some more sunscreen on." She sat on her beach towel beside him and squeezed squirts of suncream onto her arm. "Want some?" She handed Joe the plastic tube, and he applied cream to his face. With deft strokes, she spread the squishes of cream on her arm, over her face, legs, arms, and chest, and then reached down her back. "Trust Tiff not to be around when she's needed."

Joe gave a crooked grin. "Like me to rub some on

your back?"

She lay face down, and, as his long, tanned fingers smoothed cream over her neck and back, Jodie's skin tingled. She pushed her face into her towel. *If you keep that up, you'll have me moaning out loud with pleasure. What is it about you that's getting to me? You might be nice-looking, but it's not that you're all that handsome. Untrue—you're a real spunk. But, if I'm honest, personality-wise, you're a bit of a cold fish. Until today, you've hardly ever smiled or talked much. Why are you such a private person? What will it take to get to know you?"*

Sitting back on his heels, Joe checked his work. "How's that?"

"Fine, thanks. Lie down and I'll give you a treatment now."

He lay down on his front, and her hands hovered over his bare back. *Geez, my hands are starting to burn at the thought of touching you. How can I get out of putting on the cream? Stop messing about and get it over with as fast as you can.* Quickly she squirted a small pat of cream onto his back and started to smear it around in circles. Joe's flesh was warm and firm. *Boy, I've never felt the urge to kiss a guy's back before, so why even think about it now?*

Several minutes later, Jodie and Joe, with their heads under the shade of the beach umbrella, lay untouching side by side on their towels. *If I put out my hand, I could lace my fingers in yours. And, if I rolled on my side toward you and you rolled on your side toward me, we could... Phew, better to think about the warmth of the sun on my back. But it would be nice to know if you shared the same thoughts.* She squirmed, and he looked across at her. She closed her eyes. *Why don't you make a move, blow you?*

Jodie turned away from Joe onto her side. After a time, her cheek became squashed and she rolled onto her other side, bringing her face to face with him. Coloring, she went to roll back.

He put his hand on her shoulder and stopped her. "Like it here?"

Her toes curled. "It's paradise." She looked down at her towel. "Why, how do you like it?"

"I like it, but I can't stay forever."

"Why, where are you from?"

Rolling onto his back, he ignored the question and asked, "Are you from Perth?"

Why evade my question and then have the nerve to expect me to answer yours? "Yes, I've lived there all my life."

"What did you say you do besides painting?"

"I design books."

"Any I might have seen?" Jodie reeled off the names of a number of children's books and several adult books. "Haven't seen them. Got any back at camp?"

She shook her head.

"Does your boss want to publish your book of Broome paintings?"

"If I can come up with something publishable in a month."

Joe leaned closer. Jodie's mouth curled upward.

"A month? I thought Tiffany said you were going home in four days."

"She is, but not me. She's got to fly back for the start of her uni semester."

"Oh."

"What about you? When are you going home?"

He didn't answer.

"Or is Broome home now?"

"It depends."

"On what?"

"On what develops."

Jodie's mouth puckered, and she buried her face in her arms and closed her eyes.

At a light touch on her arm a few moments later, her arm tingled. Quickly she opened her eyes. Joe was sitting up and leaning over her. "I'm sorry if that sounded rude, but I have things I have to keep private at the moment. When the time comes, you'll be the first to know."

"I can't wait." She gave a forced smile. "Feel like lunch now?"

He nodded. As she opened the car fridge, Tiffany and the four young men with her abandoned the water and raced up.

While Tiffany passed around a big bag of rolls, Jodie took the lids off several containers containing ham and salad. Over lunch, the boys told stories and jokes about their travels up the west coast.

After one of Wacko's stories, Jodie wiped tears of laughter from her eyes. *He, Trent, and Pete obviously accept Ryan and Tiffany as an item and don't try to horn in on their relationship. They haven't tried to flirt with me either—not since our first meeting, anyway.* A red glow crept over her face and she groaned. *Oh no, they must think Joe and I are an item too.*

After lunch, she and Joe paddled along the beach together. They paused to look out to sea. Joe cleared his throat. "Have you got a boyfriend at home?"

She swallowed. "No, I go around in a group—less complicated that way." She took a deep breath. "What about you? Have you got a girlfriend?"

"I don't know."

"What do you mean? Either you have or you haven't."

"Okay then, I haven't."

Jodie gave him a sideways look. "Sure you haven't got a wife tucked away somewhere? And maybe a couple of children?"

"I don't think so. Come on, I'll beat you to that rock." He ran off toward a rock on the beach a hundred meters on.

Jodie groaned. "Not again," she called softly to his back. "What's with you, Mr. Mystery Man? Why can't you answer simple personal questions?"

She caught up with him at the rock and sat beside him. "I give in; you win."

"How about we swim back when we catch our breath?" Joe cupped her face in his hand and looked deep into her eyes.

Jodie trembled.

"You know, you're beautiful."

Are you going to kiss me?

Abruptly Joe took away his hand and gripped the rock so hard his knuckles showed white through his tan. "Come on. Race you back to the others."

Her eyes prickling, Jodie trailed down to the water and swam along some distance behind him. After a while, they left the water and fell into step as they walked back along the beach.

Jodie sighed. *Don't think about Joe—enjoy the*

whiteness of the sand and the brilliant turquoise of the water. But her throat ached. *Our moment of togetherness has passed. It's not fair though—you've learned so much more about me than vice versa. You must know I'm dying to find out what a person like you is doing as handyman at a caravan park.*

Joe glanced at her.

She raised her chin. "Why are you such a private person? And don't give me that enigmatic smile of yours."

He shrugged. "Perhaps you should tell me why you are such a beautiful person—on the inside as well as the outside?"

In mock disgust, she ran back into the water and swam toward Tiffany and the boys playing a ball game. As she got close to her, Jodie whispered, "Thinking of going back yet?"

"No way. We're having a camel ride along the beach at sunset."

"Joe has to get back to do his jobs at the park."

"You two go back then. I can get a lift back with Ryan and the boys. There's lots of room in the microbus."

Jodie squirmed.

"Don't be a smotherer, Jodie. I'm an adult. If I want to stay on with my friends, I can."

"I know. It's just that I feel responsible for you while we're in Broome. I'd hate anything bad to happen to you."

"Look, you've met Ryan and the boys. You know they're nice guys. There's no way they're high on dope or booze. Go off and enjoy having Joe to yourself."

"What's that supposed to mean?"

"For crying out loud, now you haven't got me for competition, it's obvious he's transferred his attention to you."

Like a fighter stunned by an unexpected punch, Jodie stared at her sister.

"Do you think you're the only ones who know about the sparks flying between you? The rest of us have just about been electrocuted every time we've gone near you. One time when you were having a heart-to-heart, Ryan sneaked up and took a photo of the two of you. He reckoned his camera nearly blew up."

Like an exasperated mother, Jodie blew out her cheeks. *Not another photo. Thank goodness Joe's not close enough to hear.*

Ryan swam up to the girls. "Who's talking about me?"

"Oh, Jodie's trying to pretend there's nothing going on between her and Joe."

"Right, and there's a shark swimming between us." He reached for Tiffany's hand. "Come on, Tiff. Let them work it out their own way, and we'll get on with whatever's going on between us." He gave Jodie a wink. The ball came their way, and Ryan and Tiffany both swam for it.

Jodie dove under the water. *Whew, I need to cool off—body and mind—after that.* She swam some backstroke and breaststroke and then swam freestyle back to Joe.

He gave her an odd look. "I thought you'd turned into a dolphin or something."

Jodie duck-dived. When she came up, Joe took a close look at her still-flushed face. "Anything I should know?"

"You tell me your secrets and I'll tell you mine."

Face as white as the surf, he dived deep, and, flicking up water with his feet, sped away from her.

Chapter 4

Tiffany brushed her hair and checked her reflection in the mirror. "Okay if we go to Cable Beach again today? The boys want to surf."

Jodie shrugged. "What about the rest of the sightseeing?"

"I thought we'd done most of it. But, if you like, we could see the croc farm this morning—it's right near Cable Beach."

"If *you* like."

As Jodie went out to the car for something for the fourth time, she sighed. *Where are you, Joe?* He emerged from his tent. "Hi, Joe. Tiff's teed us up to go to the croc farm this morning and then on to Cable Beach for the rest of the day. Like to come with us?"

"Sorry, I can't." Jodie's insides contracted. "Gilbert has lined up some maintenance jobs to keep me busy."

"Oh, I wasn't sure what your arrangement was with him."

"I clean the amenities block early every morning and move the sprinklers whenever there's a vacant site to move them to."

She nodded.

"In return I get the use of the tent, its innards, and the site free of charge. For anything extra, Gilbert pays me, and that covers my food and other living expenses."

"Oh." *Do you realize that's the most info you've ever shared about your life?* She glanced into his open tent. "Isn't the tent set-up your own?" Inside stood the old wooden table she'd seen before, an old lounge chair and a wooden high-backed kitchen chair.

"No, the maintenance guy before me set it up. He was an old guy who'd lived here since the park opened. When he passed on, Gilbert had a few fill-ins. It wasn't until I turned up that he decided he'd found the right person for the permanent job of maintenance man in this corner of the park."

Jodie frowned.

"What are you thinking?"

With a cough she mumbled, "Just wondering how you came to live in the park in the first place."

Joe's eyes narrowed. "I needed somewhere to live while I sorted a few things out. Apart from the overcrowding at peak periods and having to put up with Gilbert, it's not a bad life."

"It is very nice but, um, is it stimulating enough for you, you know, in the long term?"

"Perhaps I'm getting over a nervous breakdown from pushing myself too hard in the corporate world."

Fire engine red, Jodie spluttered, "Sorry, I didn't mean to be nosy." *Of course, that must be it—it would all add up then.*

****

A saltwater crocodile slid soundlessly into the big bush-fringed lake, and then another followed and another. With an involuntary shiver Tiffany turned to Jodie. "Had enough?"

Jodie rolled her eyes. "I guess that means you

have."

Tiffany smirked. On their way back to the car she clapped her hands. "Did I tell you Ryan and the boys are staying an extra day because of me?"

A smile lifted the corners of Jodie's mouth. "Yes, you did—several times."

"It is nice of them though, isn't it? Because they want to get around the western half of Australia in the limited time they've got, they do have to move." Tiffany took a deep breath. "It must mean Ryan likes me a lot, mustn't it?"

"Of course. Is he going to write to you when you get back to Perth?"

"He'd better. He's asked me for my address and phone number."

****

At lunch, Pete came over and sat next to Jodie under the beach umbrella. "Tiff says you're spending a month up here painting. Like to take us home to show us your etchings some time?" The boys laughed.

Jodie grinned back. *What a scream—now Joe's not around, the boys are taking more interest in me. It is good to have a flirt sometimes though. Fun, and good for the ego.*

When the group ran into the water, Jodie did a shallow dive and stood up in waist-deep water. Trent grabbed her and pulled her under. Struggling to the surface, she felt his hands tighten around her waist and she kicked and fought to get free. His hands clamped her tighter and she went under again.

A man's voice yelled, "Hoi, let her go!" Pete rushed over and pulled her up.

Spluttering and coughing, she pushed the hair back

from her eyes and her chest heaved. Tears ran down her face. "Thank you, Pete." She pulled away and blundered into shallower water.

Pete shoved Trent. "What possessed you to almost drown Jodie, you dolt?"

Jodie paddled past Tiffany and Ryan lying in warm water at the ocean's edge. Ryan looked at her tear-streaked face. "You okay, Jodie?"

"Yes, but I think I'll get out now and have a sunbake."

On the beach she quickly toweled herself dry and pulled on her top and shorts. Pink spots high on her cheeks, she muttered, "I'm not lying here in my swimsuit for that lout to eye off."

Lying with her head under the beach umbrella, she took deep breaths, and gradually her breathing slowed and became rhythmical again. Soon the warmth of the sun on her back lulled her to sleep and she dreamed of the hands of another around her waist. This time she did not fight to remove them. Instead, she lay and enjoyed the firmness of his touch and the closeness of his body.

When the others rejoined her, Trent kept to the back of the group. Jodie's nostrils flared. *Good, he's realized he's offended me. He's old enough to know girls don't like being dunked or manhandled.*

Driving back to the caravan park with Tiffany and Ryan in the back seat, Jodie glanced in her rear-vision mirror and her eyebrows shot up. *Sorry, Tiff. I'll use the outside rear-vision mirror next time. But please don't fall too hard, or you could get badly hurt. Remember it's only a holiday romance.*

That evening, like a reluctant mother, Jodie handed over her car keys to Tiffany. "Enjoy yourselves at the restaurant." Her sister backed carefully onto the roadway. In an exaggerated fashion, Ryan waved from the front passenger seat. Once they were out of sight, Jodie's smile dropped, and she walked like an abandoned puppy back into the van.

A few minutes later there was a light knock on the door. "Want to go for a walk?"

"Joe." Her face lit up with a smile as warm as a hug. "Why not?"

As they walked past an older couple sitting outside their van, Jodie waved to them. "It's a great life, isn't it?"

With a sideways look at her, Joe shook his head. "Is this what you want out of life?"

"Not now. I mean when I'm old enough for long service leave or retirement. I think it would be great to spend time traveling around Australia."

He nodded.

"What about you?" She swallowed. "Do you have any long-term goals?"

She glanced at the silent man beside her looking into the distance. *Why can't you answer me? Is there some secret you can't share with me?*

At the boom gates of the caravan park, Joe stopped. "Which way do you want to go?"

"To the right looks interesting. I haven't been that way before." They resumed walking. "What about you, Joe, do you have any long-term goals?"

"I guess so, but currently they're on hold until I sort out a few problems."

Jodie dug her nails into the palms of her hands. "What sort of problems?"

Joe shrugged. "Nothing worth sharing, not at this

stage anyway."

Biting her lip, she walked along beside him. *What does it matter to me what you want to do with yourself anyway? It's none of my business.*

Abruptly Joe stopped, grabbed Jodie by the shoulders and swung her around to face him. She trembled.

"Believe me, it's not that I don't want to tell you about myself—it's that I can't."

"Why? Why can't you?"

Thrusting her from him, he strode off ahead of her.

Well, thanks very much. No way I could keep up with you unless I ran, and I'm not doing that. Instead, she dawdled like an unhappy child behind him, and he drew farther and farther away.

When Joe was fifty or so meters ahead, a car came up behind Jodie. It honked and pulled up beside her. A carload of youths leered at her. The driver wound down his window and winked. "Hi, Dolly Parton. Wanna lift?"

"No thanks." She increased the speed of her walking. *Don't panic, whatever you do. Just keep on walking.*

Joe turned and ran back along the gravel road toward her.

Jodie took deep breaths. *Thank goodness for that.* She waved to him and called, "Time for us to go back now, darling!"

Without a word he reached her, pulled her possessively into his side and marched her back in the direction of the caravan park.

The youths in the car laughed and one mimicked, "Let's know when you want a real man, *daah-ling*, and

I'll be there for you." The car accelerated loudly, did a U-turn, and screeched away from them.

Jodie's legs buckled, and Joe stopped and turned her toward him.

"Sorry about that, Jodie. I shouldn't have left you."

She tried to smile, but her lips wobbled, and she started to shake. Joe circled his arms around her and pulled her close. She rested her head on his chest. *I can feel the warmth of your breath on my cheek, the rise and fall of your chest against mine, and the strength of your arms around me. I have never felt so safe. Please never let me go.*

Joe pulled back and turned away. "Come on, it's time we were getting back." He grabbed Jodie's hand.

Well, at least you're holding my hand. A girl could trip on this rough road. But, why, oh why do you keep knotting yourself up in your own black thoughts over and over again?

At her caravan, Joe stopped while she unlocked the door.

"Want to come in for supper?"

"No thanks, early start tomorrow. Thanks for the walk." He saluted her. "Be seeing you."

"Thanks for the walk," she echoed.

****

After thrashing around for some time in bed, Jodie fell into a restless sleep.

Someone crept into the van and turned on the light at the front of the van. "Are you awake, Jode?"

"Yeah, what is it, Tiff?" Jodie croaked groggily.

"I think I'm in love."

"Who with?"

"Ryan, of course."

Lights flashed and sirens rang in Jodie's head and she ripped open her eyes. "Don't be silly—you've only known him two days."

"I'm not being silly. Look, he's given me a ring."

Jodie shot upright. "You're not engaged."

"Of course not. It's for me to wear every day and think about him." Tiffany sat down beside Jodie.

"Hmmph."

"I've given him my gold chain so he's got a memento too. Tomorrow, will you take a photo of the two of us together, please?"

"Of course."

Like a child given the best present ever, Tiffany threw her arms around her. "Oh, isn't it just fabulous!"

"Okay, okay." Jodie extricated herself. "But take it easy, will you? Remember Ryan's off into the wilds tomorrow, and you'll be left all alone until he comes back, goodness knows when."

"No, I know when he'll be back—he has to be back in five weeks to start a new job. He's promised to write whenever he can and to look me up as soon as he gets back. Isn't that so cool?"

"Yeah, yeah, it all sounds great." She bit her lip. "Sorry, Tiff. Ryan seems to be a really nice guy, so enjoy it."

"Oh, I am, I am. And, guess what, I want you to be as happy as I am."

Jodie raised an eyebrow.

"Now I've got Ryan I'm not at all interested in Joe so I'm letting you have him. Isn't that awesome?"

"Yeah, yeah, you've already told me, remember? Whoopee-doo, big sister gets little sister's cast-offs."

Tiffany pouted. "Don't be like that. You know

what I mean. Anyway, Joe's too old for me—he'd be at least twenty-four, and Ryan's only twenty-one. You always reckoned a guy should be about two years older than the girl, so Joe should be just right for you."

****

Amid smiles and tears, Tiffany said goodbye to Ryan. As the old microbus drove off, Jodie groaned. *Uh oh, after Tiff being on a high, I'm about to cop her on a low any time now.* "Come on, Tiff; it's time we went out. Do you want to sightsee or shop for souvenirs?"

Tiffany opted to walk around Chinatown and the newer shopping areas. Jodie tagged along photographing buildings and scenes.

****

As Jodie helped Tiffany close her bulging suitcase, she gave her a side hug. "I'll be lonely without you."

"You'll be right—you've got Joe."

"Have I? He didn't come near us yesterday."

"Sorry, didn't I tell you? I bumped into him early yesterday, and he said old Gilbert had a job for him down at the shop."

"What, serving?"

"Hardly. I think it was to do with painting something. Or maybe it was plumbing?" She tossed her head. "Anyway, he said he'd be tied up all day."

"He could have come over to say hello afterwards."

"It's not as though you're really interested in him, or are you?"

Jodie turned away. "He's all right, I guess."

Tiffany smirked. "Well, don't you reckon Ryan's handsome? There's no 'I guess' about him—he's a real spunk."

As they went to lift Tiffany's case into the car, Joe

came across from shifting sprinklers. "Hi. Let me do that."

Jodie looked at him, her face as unsmiling as his. "Hi."

Tiffany took her hand off the case and stepped back. "I'm off home now. Want to come to the airport to see me off?"

Jodie held her breath.

"Sorry, Gilbert has some other joy lined up for me this morning. Have a good trip." He picked up the suitcase and placed it in the boot, gave Tiffany a smile and moved off toward the shop.

The two girls went back into the van. Arching an eyebrow, Tiffany turned to Jodie. "Have you been treading on Joe's toes?"

"Of course not."

"Well, I thought you two were getting pretty friendly down on the beach the other day. How come you've cooled it?"

"That's show business for you."

Tiffany grabbed a pretend pillow and threw it at her.

****

Standing watching Tiffany's plane get smaller and smaller, Jodie's shoulders drooped. *I feel hollowed out. I didn't think I could miss the old Tiff so much. And she's hardly left.*

As she walked back to her car, her feet dragged. *Joe, please be there when I get back.*

48

Chapter 5

Except to nod to him if they passed in the park Jodie didn't see much of Joe over the next few days. Each day she drove off to paint or to sketch scenes in pencil or charcoal. *What I'd give to have Tiff carrying on about my being a party-pooper. I love what I'm doing, but it's so lonely by myself.* She sniffed. *And Joe's a complete loss. Is it a waste of time hanging about waiting for him to take an interest in me?*

****

A week after she had waved Tiffany off, Jodie stepped out of her van. The flap on Joe's tent opened and he came out.

Jodie's throat constricted. "Hi."

"Hi."

Like a tongue-tied schoolgirl she stood looking at him and then blurted out, "Been busy?"

"Yes. Gilbert had me painting his kitchen. When I finished, he decided I did such a good job that I might as well do the whole house."

Jodie nodded.

"This is the first day I've had off in a week."

"As long as he pays you well, I guess you don't mind."

Joe snorted. "Anyway, what have you been doing with yourself since Tiff went home?"

"Painting too."

Joe grinned. "Okay if I have a look?"

She stood back and gestured for him to step inside the van. She opened her folio at her black and white sketch of the courthouse. He gave a low whistle. "Wow, I like it. No prizes for guessing what building that is."

A warmth filled the hollow inside her. She turned to her sketches of Chinatown.

Joe peered closely. "You really do have an eye for a subject. Wow, this one of the luggers stranded at Streeter's Jetty is a beauty." She held up her watercolor painting of the lugger, and he let out another low whistle. "You're not bad, are you?"

Jodie coloured. "It's my job."

As Joe took in the majestic stance of the berthed pearling lugger, its high masts reaching for the sky, he nodded. "What do you reckon your publisher will think of them?"

"Hopefully he'll like them. Since he was up here on holiday earlier this year, he's been really keen to see what I could come up with. He told me if I was prepared to take my annual holidays here to paint and sketch Broome, he'd pay for any reasonable expenses and publish my work for a good royalty."

"There's no way he'll knock these back then."

"Thanks." Her mouth wobbled. "I can do with some tender loving care just now and those words go a long way."

Watching her pack up her paintings and sketches, Joe smiled. "What's on the agenda for today?"

"I'm off to Cable Beach to see how I get on with that. A swim would be good as well. Want to come?"

"Sure, I could use a swim too."

****

As Jodie painted, Joe lay on the sand next to her. Several times he sat up and checked what she was doing. "You've really got the perspective there between the coastline and the horizon."

"Are you sure you haven't had some training in art?"

He looked away again. "Not that I know of."

She paused and looked into his face. "What training have you had?"

He looked away. "Who knows? Perhaps I was always a beach bum soaking up the sun."

Pursing her lips, Jodie applied long white stripes of paint along the long white beach stretching as far as she could see on her canvas. She stood back and studied her painting. "Reckon it'll pass muster, Professor?"

"Looks pretty good to me."

"Right. Swim time." Hand in hand, they ran into the water. They dived and splashed and swam like a couple of dolphins for half an hour.

Then together they lay on the beach. Jodie stared at the warm, tanned back beside her. *Stop itching to touch it. And don't even think about kissing it.*

Joe turned his face toward hers and opened his eyes. "What are you thinking?"

She colored and sat up. "That I'm hungry and it's time for lunch." Reaching over to her car fridge, she opened it and lifted out a plastic bag. "Fancy a roll?"

"Is that an invitation?"

She pursed her lips. "A cheese and lettuce roll."

Grinning, Joe put his hand into the bag.

After lunch he led her to the start of the Vine Thicket Walk behind Cable Beach. In a poetic trill, he read from a sign, " 'Where the red pindan soil meets the coastal dunes.' " As he and Jodie walked the two-kilometer track and attempted to identify the various species of plants along the way, they met no one. In a remote spot Jodie stopped and turned to Joe. "Doesn't it feel as though we're the only two people on earth?" Her toes tingled.

****

Most days Joe accompanied Jodie on her painting trips. While she painted, he read the papers she picked up at the newsagent's on the way. At times, he read out news items or picked out points to discuss. One day he put his theory as to the motives of a mass murderer. Jodie rolled her eyes. "I think you've missed your calling." She looked at him intently. "Or maybe you were a criminologist in an earlier life."

Without comment, Joe folded the paper and, somber-faced, lay back on the lawn in front of the building she was painting.

Her paintbrush suspended in front of her painting, Jodie studied him. *Maybe you were a policeman, a detective? Maybe you did undercover work and you're having a break? Nice thought.*

A few days later Jodie and Joe set themselves up at Riddell Beach. As Jodie slapped rust-red paint on the craggy cliffs dominating her painting, she bit her lip. "I guess you know I head for home at the end of the week."

Joe went pale and Jodie flinched.

"I guessed it was coming, but I didn't know it was quite so... I'm going to miss you, Jodie."

"I'll miss you too." She looked down at her palette and blinked away the glistening in her eyes.

****

The van shook in the wind and Jodie steadied herself against the table. *That's ominous.* She stared out at the sky dark with rainclouds. *They said to expect severe winds. But it's got dark early. I'd better have my shower before dinner instead of after.*

Almost blown off her feet returning to her van, Jodie breathed a sigh of relief as she shut out the wind. As she cut up vegetables for dinner, there came a loud rapping at the door. "It's me, Joe!" Jodie wiped her hands and hurried to the door. "They've upgraded the wind warning to a cyclone warning! There's a cyclone building up out at sea and its center is expected to just miss Broome."

Jodie sucked in her breath. "That's bad. What can we do?"

"You'll be okay—all the on-site vans are chained by a wheel to a chain embedded in concrete. I have to check them."

"What about other vans?"

"I have to chain any next to concrete blocks." He gave a wry smile. "For a fee, of course."

"What about those on the overcrowded sites?"

Joe shrugged.

"And what about the tents? What about your tent?"

"I'm taking it down and storing it and my furniture in an old shed." He coughed. "You wouldn't be able to put me up for the night, would you?"

Jodie's voice caught in her throat. "Of course, you can stay here. Come back as soon as you can. Take care."

She watched him disappear into the dark and the wind. "Take care, my darling."

****

Winds built up, and the van shook like a boat in a tempest. Above the bowls of fried rice they were eating, Joe and Jodie raised their eyebrows at each other. Several hours later as they sat talking, the power went off. Joe peered out through the curtains. "Except for the odd gas lantern, it's pitch black out there."

Jodie frowned. "I guess there's not much point in staying up. It's about my bedtime anyway. What about you?"

"Yeah, but I don't know how much sleep we'll get with this storm. I don't want to alarm you, but it might be a good idea to sleep in our clothes."

Joe made his way to a lower bunk at the front of the van and Jodie headed off to the double bed at the back. She lay down and took deep breaths. Despite the roar of the wind, the continual drum of the rain, and the shaking of the van, she fell asleep.

Suddenly, the van shook violently from side to side. Jodie sat bolt upright and gripped the side of the bed.

Screams rent the van. "No, no! The rocks are falling. Help, help!"

She jumped out of bed and lurched her way to the front bunk. "It's okay, Joe, it's okay!" Joe sat flailing his arms around. She tried to put her arms around him.

He held his hands to his eyes. "No, no! The rocks, the rocks! They're going to hit me! They're going to hit me!"

A big gust of wind rocked the van and flung Jodie hard against Joe. He pushed her off.

"Joe, it's me, Jodie! Wake up, wake up!"

"Jodie, is that you?" He threw his arms around her and buried his head in her chest.

She brushed his hair back from his sweating face. "Take it easy, Joe. Take deep breaths. It's okay. It's going to be okay."

He stopped shaking and pulled back from her. "What's happening?"

"It's the cyclone. Don't you remember?"

Another huge gust shook the van and sent Jodie sprawling on Joe's bunk and into the wall. "Ow, that hurt!" She picked herself up and rubbed her head.

The van rocked violently again. Joe and Jodie grabbed for handholds.

"Quick, come into my bed with me, Joe. It will be safer there." Tripping and feeling their way along the wall, the two made their way to the double bed and clambered in.

Her breathing coming in short spasms, she lay on her back and took deep breaths. The storm whined and screeched about her and the roof creaked and scraped. "Oh, my god, the roof's going to take off any minute!"

Joe's arms enveloped her. "Hush, everything will be all right. But will you be okay if we have to make a run for it?"

"Yes." She let out a sob. "But I like our chances better in here than out there."

Joe kissed her forehead. He pulled her closer and they lay locked against each other while the storm raged around them.

After some time, the wind and rain started to abate. Jodie pulled herself away from Joe and lay on her back again. He picked up her hand and kissed it.

She trembled. *Don't think about the warmth and safety of lying in Joe's arms.* He kissed the inside of her palm. *Oh, Joe, you don't know how much I want to roll over and have you hold me tight again. What I'd give to feel your body full length against mine.*

"Joe," she whispered. *Don't. Don't you dare search around for some nonsensical reason to keep him here in your bed now the worst of the cyclone has passed.*

"Yes?"

"What were you dreaming about when you called out in your sleep?"

"What did I say?"

"You were screaming something about rocks and them going to hit you."

"You're joking."

"No. Were you dreaming about being in an avalanche or something?"

Like a patient who had undergone brain surgery, Joe rolled his head sideways and guided Jodie's hand to the back of his head. "Feel that—very gently now…. What can you feel?"

"A lump—a big lump. Where did it come from?"

"No idea, but I do know it was a jolly lot larger when I first felt it."

"What did the doctor say?"

"Nothing—I haven't been near one."

"That's silly. Why not?"

He gripped her hands. "Can I trust you?"

"Of course you can—you know that."

He took a deep breath. "You know you've been puzzled why someone like me is bumming around in a place like Broome with no relatives or friends, no proper job, no apparent means of support, and no apparent ambition or direction in life?"

Jodie colored. "Have I been that obvious?"

"Don't be embarrassed. It's a compliment really." Joe kissed the tips of her fingers and her toes curled.

Keep that up and the ache inside me will grow so huge, I'll have to throw myself at you.

"You don't happen to want a passenger back to Perth, do you?"

Jodie's breath caught in her throat "Why, who wants a ride? Tiff was supposed to be flying up to drive back with me. But now she reckons she can't spare the time from uni. Dad suggested I sell the car up here and fly home but even if I could find a buyer, I've got too much gear to even think about that. So I was going to drive back by myself with as few stops as possible."

"That's dangerous. I'm surprised you've even thought about it."

"I wasn't going to stop off and sightsee by myself."

"If you take me as a passenger, it won't be an issue."

As Joe pulled her into the crook of his shoulder, Jodie's insides performed somersaults. "Hey, you haven't explained to me about that big egg on the back of your head yet. What gives?"

"I don't know."

"So you said, but there's no way you could collect that and not know about it."

"Well, I certainly knew about it afterwards."

"Pardon?"

"I think I must have been hit in an avalanche, been in a car accident or been clobbered."

Jodie swallowed. "You'll have to do better than that. What can you remember before the accident—where were you, what were you doing, that sort of thing?"

"I don't know. I honestly and truly don't know."

Jodie's brow furrowed. "You mean you've lost your memory—you're suffering from amnesia?" She stared into his troubled face. "Good grief, Joe, it's all coming together to support what you're saying—your obvious intelligence that's so at odds with your lifestyle, your lack of a job in keeping with your abilities, your apparent lack of ambition, your lack of friends, your 'dampened-down' personality."

"Thanks for the reference."

She gave a sick grin.

His face darkened. "I thought if I took it slow and easy it would all come back to me, but it hasn't."

"Why didn't you see a doctor?"

"You'd think I was mad if I told you."

"Try me."

"I have this gut feeling I'm in some great danger. So, if I go to a doctor who ends up making my situation public, whoever my enemy is will come and get me."

"You're being paranoid."

He pulled his arm away from under her head. "I knew you wouldn't understand—I couldn't expect you or anyone else to for that matter."

She took a deep breath. "If you want to come back to Perth with me, you can, but only on the condition you let my father have a look at your head when we get there. He's a doctor, and he'll be able to help you or send you to someone who can."

Joe didn't answer, but rolled to the far side of the bed.

After some time without physical or mental contact, Jodie rolled away as far as she could on her side of the bed. Sporadic gusts of wind shook the van, and the wind howled. Eventually she slept.

Light streamed into the van, and excited voices called to each other outside. Jodie stirred. *What's going on? What happened about the cyclone?* She reached out next to her. Her hand fell onto a cold empty sheet. *Where are you, Joe?* She jumped out of bed and ran to the door.

Debris was strewn everywhere and one small van nearby lay overturned. People milled around it. A neighbor ran over. "Are you okay?"

Jodie nodded.

"Yes, thanks, but what about whoever was in that van?"

"They're good—only because they spent the night at a motel though. They couldn't get a van site with a concrete slab with chains here, and they weren't prepared to take the risk of staying in an unanchored van."

Jodie shook her head. "Just as well."

In the middle of a group of men around the overturned van, Joe was pointing to a rope attached to it. "Right, all heave on the count of three. One, two, three!" The men heaved. The van lurched upwards and rocked crazily. Fellow caravanners watched on. The van landed on its wheels. The crowd let out a roar and broke into spontaneous clapping.

Jodie smiled. *I always knew you had it in you, Joe. You worked out what needed to be done and took charge—you're a leader.*

****

Broken palms, uprooted trees, and flattened bushes lined the road to the shops. As she drove along, Jodie let out a whistle. Then she passed several unroofed houses and other damaged houses. Workers were placing canvas sheeting or poly tarp over exposed sections of walls and roofs.

Uh-oh, this area must have really copped it. How lucky Joe and I were. And how lucky I was to have Joe with me during it all. She pulled up and took several photos. *Strictly for my records. No way am I painting the aftermath of this savage destruction.*

****

As she walked past the laundry, Jodie glanced in. Joe was mopping the flooded floor. Her pulse quickened. "Come and have a sandwich with me when you're finished, Joe?"

"Give me fifteen minutes."

At the door of the van, he stepped out of his gumboots. Over lunch they swapped news of their mornings. Jodie's brow furrowed. "If Gilbert had been better prepared, was any of the damage avoidable?"

Joe nodded. "I can't take much more of the way he runs this place. Just think—soon I'll never have to see the boss from hell again."

"Have you told him you'll be finishing up on Friday?"

Joe laughed. "Yes, and he wasn't too thrilled. I think he had visions of me doing all the dirty work cleaning up after the storm."

Reaching over to touch his sleeve, Jodie looked searchingly into his face. "When we get back to Perth, remember you're letting my dad have a look at you."

Joe's jawline tightened, and a tiny nerve throbbed in his cheek. "I'll think about it."

Chapter 6

Before it was quite light, Joe headed out of the caravan park. Peeping out the van window, Jodie grinned. *With your hair hidden under that peaked cap and that small pack on your back, even Gilbert wouldn't recognize you now.* A short while later Jodie dropped her van key into the key box at the park office and headed off in her car.

A kilometer or so down the road, she caught up with Joe and pulled over. "Gee, I'd have to be mad picking up a low life like you with three days' growth on your face."

Without answering, Joe quickly threw his pack into the small space Jodie had reserved for it over the back seat and covered it. Then he climbed into the passenger seat and slipped down onto the floor.

Jodie shook her head. "This cloak and dagger stuff is starting to get at me. Are you sure it's really necessary?"

"I told you before, it's gut instinct. Just forget I'm here and get us out on the highway before anyone sees me. Please."

Frowning, she pulled out and negotiated the small amount of traffic around at that time of the morning. Once they were on the Great Northern Highway and had it to themselves, Joe sat in the passenger seat.

Jodie glanced at his serious face. "What do you

think there is to be wary of?"

"You work it out. How likely am I to have got a gigantic bump on the back of my head from a car accident or a fall? If I did get it from some trauma, why didn't I regain consciousness in a smashed-up car or a hospital or at the bottom of a cliff?"

"Where did you come to?"

"In the middle of nowhere under a pile of leaves and branches."

White-faced, Jodie gripped the steering wheel tighter. "Y-you never told me."

"What, told you that some person or persons unknown had obviously tried to cover up what they thought was my dead body?" He stared at her face. "Come on, what would you have thought if I'd told you that?"

"I-I- don't know."

"That I was some sort of druggie who'd been done over because of a drug deal that had turned sour?"

Jodie gulped. "I never said that." *But just the same, my mind's racing with all sorts of mad thoughts. They're so mad and bad, I don't know what to think. For the first time I feel scared, and this time it's for me, for myself. Here I am out in the Australian Outback with someone I might be wildly attracted to, but someone I hardly know and whose background I certainly don't know. Where the heck does that leave me if you're not the lovely Joe I've grown to think you are? Thank goodness you can't read my mind. Just as well I rang Mum and Dad last night to tell them what I'm doing every day for the next week or so.* She cleared her throat. "Have you come up with any theories yourself?"

"Not really. But I've definitely rejected theories of accidents and am concentrating on those where someone's intentionally tried to do away with me."

"You don't think a hitchhiker might have brained you before stealing your car?"

"Possibly, but what would I be doing driving around up here by myself anyway?"

"Where exactly were you when you came to?"

"On some god-forsaken track somewhere between here and Port Hedland."

Jodie smothered a gasp. "Then why did you head north rather than head south where you might get more help?"

"The first car that came along and stopped was heading north. So I took the lift I was offered."

"What did the people in the car make of you?"

"What, with dried blood down the back of my head and on my clothes?" Joe smiled without mirth. "The people were Aborigines heading for Broome. Even though the car was packed, they made room for someone in trouble. They decided I'd been a hitchhiker who'd been in a fight with some drunken louts who'd given me a lift, pinched my gear, and then pitched me out of the car."

"Perhaps that's what really did happen."

Joe gave a grim smile. "Maybe, but I've got no gut feeling for the story."

"What were you wearing when you were found?"

He pointed to his pants. "These jeans and a navy-blue tee shirt."

Jodie nodded.

"The guys who gave me a lift were great. They took me to their camp, cleaned me up, gave me a clean tee shirt, fed me, looked after me until I was halfway *compos mentis* and then drove me into Broome."

"You owe them a lot."

"My life. But for their sakes, I've made a point of steering clear of them ever since. I don't want them getting involved in the mystery, especially if it has nasty repercussions."

Jodie's breath came out in a rasp. "How did you come to end up at Gilbert's?"

"One of the women at the Aboriginal camp told the men she'd heard the old guy who'd helped Gilbert out had died. She reckoned Gilbert wasn't happy with the others he'd tried out and that the job could be up for grabs."

"So you walked in and got it?"

"Yes, literally."

After a couple of hours' driving, Jodie stopped for a break. As they did stretches, Joe gave her a cheeky grin. "Like me to take a turn at the wheel?"

She pulled a disbelieving face. "Sure you know how to drive?"

"I won't know until I get started. But I have one of those gut feelings that I can. Trust me with your car?"

More to the point, can I trust you not to whip off somewhere with or without me in it? Like a prim aunt, she sat in the passenger seat and gave him instructions. He turned on the ignition. Immediately the car purred into life and he pulled out onto the highway. He beamed. "Howzat?"

Jodie grinned and relaxed. Before long she dozed off. Suddenly, the car slowed, and she shook herself awake. "What's up?"

A pulse twitched in Joe's cheek. "I think that's

near where I was dumped. The guys who picked me up told me roughly where they picked me up, and it was near here. They reckoned I was so weak and dopey when they found me, I couldn't have got far along the highway from where I'd been attacked."

At a track off to the right of the highway, the car came to an abrupt stop. Jodie took a deep breath. "Do you want to drive down that track?"

"If you're okay with it, I'd like to drive down it far enough not to be seen from the highway. Then I'd like to walk down it. Feel like coming with me? I don't think it'll be far."

Jodie nodded. *What are you letting yourself in for, you silly girl?*

Joe turned off the road, drove along the track through light bush for about twenty meters, and pulled up. "No good going any farther unless you want to get your car scratched with the heavier undergrowth."

With a quick look around, he climbed out and got his backpack. Jodie picked up her camera and locked the car.

Without speaking, she and Joe made their way along the rough track. She clenched and unclenched her hands. *How crazy must I be?* "Any car tracks or footprints would be gone by now, wouldn't they, Joe? How long ago was it anyway?"

"Two months. So I know I'm just kidding myself there'll be signs—especially after the cyclone. But I do feel I have to go over everything I know for even the tiniest clue."

About a hundred meters along the track, an offshoot track branched off into slightly denser bushland. Joe headed down the offshoot track. After pausing to look around in all directions, Jodie followed. Her body gave an involuntary shiver.

Joe stared hard at her. "You okay? You've gone very quiet."

Forcing a smile, she nodded. But, as he took her hand and gave it a squeeze, he frowned. "Then how come your hand's so cold, when the temperature must be at least thirty degrees?"

Jodie pulled her hand away and walked on.

Suddenly, Joe stopped. Under some bushes to the side of the track lay a hollow. Beside it lay a scattered pile of broken branches and dead leaves. Joe raised his hand. "Don't move." He bent down and studied the ground. "This is the spot, I'm sure."

Her voice caught in her throat. "What, of what could have been your grave?"

Like a detective's assistant, Jodie took out her camera and took photos.

Joe pointed. "Look, over here you can see where the bushes have been damaged as though a vehicle's turned around here."

She took another photo.

Joe beckoned her over to where he was squatting. "Look at this under this tree—a faint tire mark that hasn't been wiped out by the storms." Quickly he pulled off his pack and undid it. Her mouth open, Jodie watched as he took out a packet of quick-acting plaster of Paris, a bowl, and a bottle of water. After mixing up a small quantity of plaster of Paris and water in the bowl, he poured the mixture into the tire print.

Jodie shook her head. *Wow, you're a different Joe I'm seeing in action now.*

Her teeth started to chatter and she pressed her lips

together. Joe rushed over and put his arm around her shoulders. "You poor kid, fancy involving you in this detective work."

Nervously she looked around.

"Hey, no need to worry about anyone else being here. It stands to reason no one in his right mind is going to return to the scene of his crime. Anyway, he thinks I'm dead."

"Murdered." She shuddered again.

On the way back to the car, Jodie constantly looked back over her shoulder. In the car, her eyes met Joe's as she checked the rear-vision mirrors for the fourth time in two minutes as he drove along. She gave a silly laugh. "You'll have me as neurotic as you are soon."

He squeezed her knee and she rubbed her forehead. "What do you reckon your plaster cast will prove?"

He frowned. "I'm not sure, but if I can get access to tire treads, I might be able to work out what sort of a vehicle would use one that would make such a mark. If I know what sort of vehicle carried me into the bush, it might help me to recall how I came to be in it."

"You're sure you were attacked in the bush? You don't think you might have been hit elsewhere and brought here for disposal? Oh, gosh, what am I saying!" Another shudder ran through her.

"I couldn't say at this stage, but the more clues I get, the more chance I've got of putting together the various pieces of the jigsaw puzzle and working out what happened. Who knows? Something might jog my memory."

Grim-faced, Jodie nodded and went quiet. After a time, she looked over at him. "You know, I've been thinking. You don't think you could be a policeman or a detective who ran foul of a criminal?"

"The thought did cross my mind."

"What sort of business could you possibly have had at Port Hedland?"

"Who knows? Maybe it was something to do with smugglers of pearls, opals, drugs, you name it. Anything could go on at a big port like Port Hedland or along an isolated coastline like we've got along here."

"Well, as long as you're the goodie and not the baddie in all this." Her voice faltered.

"Hey, what's that supposed to mean?"

"Joke."

"It had better be. I've got enough problems trying to get it together without my only friend in the world having doubts about me."

With a tremulous smile she patted Joe's knee. Leaving one hand on the wheel, he covered her hand with his free hand. Her hand twitched.

Some hours later Joe drove the car into a caravan park at South Hedland.

When Jodie returned from the office, she waved a key. "They were out of on-site vans so I had to get us a cabin." She pointed in the direction of a new-looking unit.

Joe reddened. "Sorry I haven't much money to share costs. When I get back on my feet, I promise I'll pay you back."

"Don't be silly—my boss is paying for most of it. Even if he wasn't, you know I don't expect anything. You got me out of a hole by being my company home, remember?"

Jodie opened the door of the cabin. A double bed dominated the room. She sucked in her breath. A single bed stood against the far wall and she let out her breath.

Joe glanced around. "Hmm, luxury, eh?"

She followed his gaze to a television set on a shelf.

The two carried in their overnight gear and unpacked. Joe glanced at the clock. "We've got an hour or two before tea. Fancy a quick trip to Port Hedland?"

"What for?"

An innocent look on his face, he opened the cabin door and bowed low. "I thought you might like a look around."

"You mean you'd like to have a look around. You've got that gleam in your eye again. You're on to something, aren't you?"

"Just trying to awaken dormant memories, that's all."

As they drove around the narrow island on which the town was built, Jodie glanced at the tourist literature. "See how this long causeway connects the mainland to the island?"

Joe nodded.

"There are three of these causeways. And did you know the port handles more tonnage than any other Australian port?"

Joe grinned. "I do now."

"If we had time, we could come down and watch them load iron ore from some of the world's biggest mines onto the world's biggest ore carriers."

"Sounds like 'big' is the operative word."

"Yes, and it's even big for salt. They export about two million tons of salt a year."

"Sounds a bit tame after watching that endlessly long train carrying iron ore that we saw snaking along earlier."

"It says here the trains from Newman to Port Hedland are 2.89 kilometers long."

"I said 'big' was the operative word!"

****

Jodie sat at the table opposite Joe and picked up a chip. "After a long day's car travel, eating take-away fish and chips is my idea of bliss."

"Don't forget to add, 'And watching television.' " Joe pointed the remote control. "Hope you don't mind, but it's seven o'clock, and I want to keep up with the news."

Her mouth full of chip, Jodie nodded.

A police officer appeared on the screen. Joe leaned forward and Jodie looked over at him. *Gee, you certainly get focused anytime anything connected with crime comes up. What does that suggest about your past?*

Later he sprawled on the couch next to her watching a police drama. A warm glow enveloped her. *Do married couples feel the way I feel now? Would a young wife want to lie down beside her husband for a cuddle and vice versa?* A blush spread across her face.

Before the characters on the television came up with clues, Joe pointed clues out to her. At the end of the program, he turned off the television. "What a hopeless lot! The detectives in that show needed basic lessons in being detectives."

"Why, what do you reckon they should have done?"

"For starters, the guy with the moustache didn't know how to go about an investigation. He didn't use a glove or even a handkerchief when he picked up the murder victim's glass. That reduced the chance of successfully checking it for fingerprints."

"How do you reckon you should go about an investigation?" Jodie held her breath.

"First you cordon off the crime scene so people don't go trampling all over it before you've had a chance to thoroughly search it for any clues. Then–" Catching sight of her intent look, he broke off. "Hey, listen to me. Am I a crime show freak or what?"

"Or what?"

"No, just because I know a bit about crime and detectives and crimes doesn't make me a cop or a detective. It's just common sense."

Jodie laughed. "You've gone red. You think you could be a cop or a detective, don't you?"

That night, Jodie got into the double bed and Joe took the single. During the night she thrashed about. *Oh, Joe, don't you know my body's aching to feel your hard maleness beside me like I felt it the night of the cyclone.*

Suddenly, Joe yelled out. "No, no, don't hit me!" She jumped out of bed and ran to him. She climbed into bed beside him and held him close.

He pushed her away. "No, no!"

"Hush, hush, it's all okay." For several minutes, Jodie held him and rocked him against her. As he calmed down, she breathed out a silent whistle.

"Gee, Jodie, I'm sorry. You know, that time I had the name of the guy who brained me on the tip of my tongue, and I almost got a picture of him."

"You're sure you were hit?"

"Oh yes, no doubt about it at all."

"Wonderful. Your memory must be on the point of returning—just give it time."

Jodie went to climb out of the bed but Joe pulled her back and lay her down. Then he lifted himself above her. As he lowered himself down on top of her, Jodie pushed at him weakly. "No, Joe, not like this. The time's not right." All her senses pulsating wildly, she surrendered to his long passionate kiss. *Not fair, Joe— my heart is bursting.*

She buried her face in his warm chest "Oh, Joe, I think I must be falling in …"

"Don't say it!" He pushed her away and rolled off her.

As though paralyzed, Jodie lay motionless for some moments. Then she sat up, her face stiff. "I'm sorry, I must be confused—I thought something must have been mutual."

His back to her, Joe pressed his fingers into his forehead. "Hasn't it ever occurred to you I might be married?"

"Noooo!" Her face blazing red, Jodie threw back the bedclothes and jumped out of the bed.

Joe turned and lunged for her, grabbed her wrist and held it tight. After a few moments he dropped it. "I'm sorry."

"What for?"

"You know—about my 'might be married.' "

"Oh that. I thought you might have had a gut feeling about that too."

"Don't be like that."

"Why not? You knew you could drive a car and you certainly knew how to handle one once you got into the driver's seat. What's so different about knowing how to behave in bed?"

"Very different, if you must know."

"Well, have you done it before or not?"

"I don't know."

"Well, I haven't, and I'm as sure as hell sure I'd know if I had or not."

"My gut feeling tells me I haven't, but you mean so much to me, I want to be sure." He took her hand.

A tear leaked out of her eye. *Don't say that unless you're free—I couldn't bear it if you're not.* Jodie extricated her hand. "Right, then, it looks as though it's a stalemate until you get your memory back. See you in the morning." She turned away and returned to the double bed.

****

Early the next morning Jodie and Joe packed the car and set off down the highway again. An hour into the trip, Joe took the wheel. Jodie glanced across at him. *Why do you have to be so complicated? Why do you have to carry all this baggage?* She touched his arm. "How did you come up with the name Joe?"

"One of the Aborigines who saw me staggering along the highway called out, 'Hey, Joe, you want a lift or what?'"

She laughed. "I might have known there was no gut feeling leading you to choose your name."

"No, and I've had no sense of identity to give me one since."

"Let's look at what we know about you. Because of your looks, we know you're very likely to be of European and not Asian or Aboriginal descent and you speak like an Australian but not like an Ocker Australian. And you're tanned with dark curly hair and brown eyes. Any idea whether you're from a British or maybe a Greek, Italian, or Jewish background?"

"I have thought about it but there's nothing other than my looks and Aussie accent to go on. I wasn't wearing a cross around my neck or anything like that. If you're interested, I've been circumcised so it's not likely I'm Continental."

Jodie blushed.

"Could be Jewish, of course. But most likely I'm an Anglo-Saxon Australian. Agree?"

She shrugged. "Any fillings or false teeth?"

"Gee, who's supposed to have been the detective in an earlier reincarnation? No to the false teeth, yes to the fillings. But how are they going to help me?"

"If you're listed somewhere as a missing person, you might be able to go through the records of any likely missing person and check your fillings off against his."

Joe tried not to laugh. "You're such a sweetie. I'm not dead nor unrecognisable. Wouldn't it be easier just to go through photos of missing persons and check for likenesses?"

"Oh, you're impossible!" Jodie swatted his leg with her hand. "If you're so clever, you throw up some ideas."

"When we get back, I want to do some research."

"Such as?"

"I want to go through all the newspapers that were published just before and just after I lost my memory."

"Why didn't you do it when you first got to Broome?"

"One, I was pretty *non compos mentis* for a couple of weeks after I was found and the Aborigines cared for me. Two, Gilbert ran me off my feet catching up on all the maintenance jobs that had been allowed to run down after his old maintenance man died. To top it off, he presumed I was on unemployment benefits and apparently living like a lord, so he didn't advance me any money. That meant I had to do something to earn money as fast as I could."

"Did you have any money on you when you were found?"

"Not a cent. There wasn't a thing in any of my pockets."

"How did you manage?"

"I had to put the hard word on Gilbert for an advance. All he'd come up with was five dollars, so I lived pretty much on bread and vegemite and water and the odd banana for a fortnight."

"Oh, Joe. And did you get unemployment benefits finally?"

"How could I? No name, no address and running scared for my life. No way—I just lay like an injured bird waiting until I could build up the energy and reserves to take stock of my life again." He turned and flashed a smile at her. "I must admit though, after about a month, a little guardian angel turned up, and she proved to be a bit of an asset."

Jodie placed her hand on his leg, and then quickly removed it again.

Joe grinned. "Want to try to get to Carnarvon tonight?"

"That's more than eight hundred fifty kilometers in a day."

"We've got two drivers, remember? We could make it to Perth tomorrow if we really wanted."

"Perth's about nine hundred kilometers from Carnarvon."

Joe shrugged. "So…"

****

After three days of hard driving, they drove into the Perth suburb where Jodie lived with Tiffany and their parents. It was dark when she pulled into their drive at nine o'clock.

At the same time as she put her key in the lock, she pressed the buzzer. She opened the door. "Only us!"

A surprised face appeared around the lounge room door. Its owner, a slim woman in her late forties, ran and threw her arms around her. "Jodie! We weren't expecting you until tomorrow at the earliest. Why didn't you ring?"

"Mum, this is Joe. Joe, my mother, Beth Winter."

A tall balding man with a graying beard rushed up from behind Beth and embraced Jodie in a bear hug. "For goodness sake, Jodie!"

She hugged him back and then held his arm and turned him to face Joe. "Joe, this is my father, Tom Winter."

Tiffany came catapulting up the passage and gave her sister a bone-crunching hug. Then she turned to Joe. "And who is this insalubrious person traveling incognito with a week's growth on his face?"

He gave her a grin. "Hi, Tiff. Misbehaving yourself?"

With a friendly punch, she grinned back. "Guess what? Ryan rang on Sunday. They were at Tennant Creek then. By now they should be at Alice Springs. Isn't it wonderful—Ryan'll be back in Perth in a few weeks!" She squeezed Jodie's arm. "Come on, come and tell us all your news."

Beth stepped between them. "First things first.

Have you and Joe had dinner, Jodie?"

"Yes, thanks, Mum, we stopped off along the way."

"Then I'll put the kettle on and bring in some biscuits for supper then."

From his armchair by the fire, Tom listened to his two daughters exchanging news. When Joe joined in, Jodie glanced at her father, and then threw him a beseeching look. *Oh, Dad, please don't judge Joe by his appearance. He's not always this unkempt. Please stop making it so obvious you're summing him up. Please."*

Tom smiled. "How was the trip down, Joe?"

With a silent whistle, Jodie ran out to the kitchen to her mother. Quickly she filled her in on what was going on with Joe.

That night Jodie curled up in the fetal position in her own bedroom. *Thank you, big brother Kieran, for moving out of home. Wow, who'd ever have thought the nicest guy I've ever met would be sleeping in your old room next to mine tonight.*

Chapter 7

The following morning, Jodie walked into the kitchen. Her father looked up from drinking his tea and reading the paper.

"Dad, I need to talk to you about Joe. He was hit on the head, and he's suffering from amnesia."

"Yes, your mum gave me a bit of a rundown, but I need to know a lot more." A serious look on his face, Tom heard his daughter through. "That's an incredible story. Joe should have got help immediately. I wish you'd told me last night. The more time goes by, the less chance he's got of ever regaining the memory he's lost."

Her face ashen, Jodie gulped. "What do you think he should do?"

"Be examined by a doctor for a start and then undergo comprehensive tests to get an accurate diagnosis."

"Then?"

"Get on to Missing Persons and, if necessary, go public. Get his photo on the front page of every major newspaper and on the television news programs. Within twenty-four hours, he should at least know who he is and what's likely to have happened to him."

"No, Dad. He thinks he's got enemies, so doesn't want any publicity."

Tom raised his eyebrows.

"Couldn't you check him over yourself—please?"

With a tap on the open door, Joe stepped into the kitchen. "Hi. Mind if I join you?"

Tom gave him a nod. "Morning, Joe. Sleep well?"

"Like the proverbial log."

"Good. Jodie tells me you suffered an unknown injury about nine or ten weeks ago, and you'd like me to have a look at it. Is that right?"

Relief flashed across Joe's face. "If you wouldn't mind."

"I should get you to come around to my surgery later this morning, but in case there's something that's obviously urgent, I think I'd better take a quick look at you right now. Would you like to come into the lounge room with me, please? I'll just grab my medical case and be with you in a moment."

Ten minutes later Joe returned. "Your dad wants a specialist friend to have a look at me as soon as possible. He said he'll want scans done."

"What about trying to identify you?"

"He seems to think my gut feelings about danger are possibly related to some paranoia brought on by my hit on the head. However, he is prepared to accept I don't want to go public."

"That doesn't explain your grave of leaves. What's he suggest you do anyway?"

"He's in there now ringing up some contact in the police force to see if anyone fitting my description is listed in their Missing Persons files."

"Couldn't that be dangerous for you?"

They looked up as Tom came back into the room. "Right, Joe, I've just made an appointment for you to get your scans done this morning. Jodie, I've made an appointment for you this afternoon to go through Missing Person files to see if you can find a mention of Joe there."

"Thanks, Dad—that's great."

****

Plowing through scores of photos at Missing Persons, Jodie laid her hand on her stomach. *These butterflies must be telling me I'm about to uncover something momentous. I do hope so.* A few minutes later she turned a page and a photo of Joe's face stared back at her. *Oh, Joe, Joe. You're clean-shaven and your beautiful curls are cut off but it's you. Thank goodness, someone has reported you missing."*

Quickly she copied the details, her eyes widening as she did so. *Detective Constable Marc O'Connors, aged twenty-five.* All the dates, including the date of Joe's disappearance, fitted. She jotted them down. *What a pity there's not a photocopier nearby I could use without anyone noticing.* She breathed deeply. *Boy, I feel like a volcano about to explode. Marc, my Joe is Marc.*

She hurried past the official who had directed her to the files. "Thanks for your help." *Please don't stop me to ask me how I got on.*

He smiled and threw her a wink.

Back at her car, she opened the driver's door and climbed in. An inquiring look on his face, Joe looked at her from the passenger seat. "Hello, Marc."

"Marc?"

Her face splitting with a Cheshire Cat grin, she nodded. "That's right, Marc, Marc O'Connors. Ring any bells?"

Jodie passed her notes across to Joe/Marc. He

looked at them and let out a low whistle. "Detective Constable, how do you like that?"

"Hang on to your hat—we're going visiting now."

"Where to?"

"Somewhere that should bring back memories."

As they drove along, Joe/Marc frowned. "You know, while I was waiting for you, I surreptitiously watched all the comings and goings of people going about their business, and nothing rang a bell. No gut feeling. Nothing."

Thirty minutes later, Jodie pulled up at a neat brick house in a quiet suburban street. "Look familiar?"

Joe/Marc shook his head.

While he stayed in the car, Jodie rang the front doorbell of the house. She tried several times and waited several minutes. No one answered. She went around the back and knocked but there was still no answer.

Jodie returned to the car. "This is your home address. Perhaps your mother works, or perhaps she's gone shopping."

Joe/Marc shook his head. "My mother!" He frowned. "Perhaps I don't live with my mother."

Jodie's mouth curved downwards. "Well, perhaps your wife works, or perhaps she's gone shopping."

Joe/Marc's mouth curved downwards.

An attractive dark-haired young woman and a matronly middle-aged woman came out of the house across the street and hurried over to the car.

The older woman looked at Jodie. "Excuse me, I live here. Were you looking for me?"

Wow, you must be Joe/Marc's mum, you're so like him for looks. Jodie swallowed and took a quick glance at Joe/Marc's face. *Your mouth's dropped open, but there's no sign of recognition.* Tears welled in her eyes.

Suddenly, the younger woman glanced at the man in the car. "Marc!" She threw open the car door and pulled Joe/Marc out. Then she threw her arms around him and kissed him.

Jodie paled and her knees buckled. *At least you turned your face just in time for the kiss to land on your cheek instead of your mouth.*

The younger woman turned to the older one. "Oh, Eve, it's Marc—he's come home to us!"

Tears rolling down her face, the older woman held her arms out as though in a dream. Marc went to her and allowed her to embrace him. With Eve on one arm and the younger woman clinging to the other, he was propelled towards the house. Jodie followed.

Where does this leave me? And what about the "enemy" Joe/Marc's so concerned about? Like a CIA agent, she glanced around and then followed the others into the house.

Eve gestured to Marc to sit down on the couch, and she sat next to him. Like a bird, the younger woman swooped to sit on his other side.

Jodie shook her head. *Poor Joe/Marc, aren't you the picture of confusion?*

Her long hair brushing his shoulder, the younger woman clutched his arm. "Don't you know me either, Marc? I'm Linda. You've known me since I was born. You were my hero walking me to school, protecting me from the bullies when you were in Year Two and I was in Prep." Like a possessive wife, she tried to link her arm through Marc's. He pulled away.

A polite smile fixed on her face, Jodie stared at her.

Why can't you take the hint and go home, Linda?

Eve put her hand on her son's arm. "Oh Marc, I guess you and...and..."

"Jodie."

"Yes, of course, so you said before. I'm sorry, I'm so excited at seeing you again, I can't seem to get myself together. I'm so glad it was my day off from the clinic today. It would have been terrible if I'd been at work when you came. Come out to the kitchen with me, Marc, and I'll make us all a cup of tea."

As they left the room together, Eve patted Marc's arm. "I've been keeping your special shortbreads for when you came home."

Linda went to jump up but Jodie waved her down. "Probably best to leave them alone to get re-acquainted again."

"But..."

"Doctor's orders." *Hope I'll be forgiven for telling a white lie to protect Joe/Marc.*

Pouting, Linda stayed seated. "How do you know Marc?"

"Um, we met about a month after he lost his memory. I've just been helping him find out who he is."

"Where did you meet him?"

"Look, I think I'd better leave all that for Joe, uh, Marc, to tell you. He's still not in good condition medically and I don't want to do or say anything that might worsen his condition."

"But how could...?"

"What about you, Linda? How well do you know Joe, er Marc?"

"Like I said, I've known him all my life. When I was little, he was like the big brother I never had. Then when we got older…well, take a look at that photo over there."

A younger Joe/Marc in a dinner-suit and a younger Linda in a full-length white deb dress stood smiling at her. "Doesn't he look handsome? All the girls would have killed to have him as a partner but he chose me."

Or, more like it, you put the hard word on him. Jodie walked over to the photo. "I like your gown."

"Yes, lovely, isn't it? Marc's mum made it for me. She's like a second mother to me."

Make sure you rub it in, and don't think I don't know what you're trying to do. Well, I won't be warned off because something doesn't quite jell here. You're not the girl for Marc, and he'd have to be blind not to see it.

Linda pointed in the direction of her house. "Why, Eve's just been over to my place showing me how to finish off a dress I'm making." She broke off. "Marc." Jumping up she ran to him, almost knocking over the tray with cups of tea that he was carrying. "Have you remembered me yet, darling?"

Jodie's ears pricked up and Marc's reddened.

"Sorry, Linda. For starters I'm still working on remembering Mum, I'm afraid."

"Oh, Marc, and here we were about to make our engagement public."

"Engagement?" His hoarse cry filled the room.

Jodie closed her eyes. *Please say she's got it wrong.*

"Yes, on my twenty-third birthday next month. You must remember that."

Eve came in. "Oh, Linda, you naughty girl, you didn't even give me a hint." She put down the sugar bowl and biscuits she was carrying and went over to kiss her. "What a lovely day this has turned out to be— first I get Marc back and then I hear you and Marc are to be married. I'm so happy."

Marc dumped the tray of drinks on a coffee table. "Whoa, whoa!"

Jodie cringed inside. *Stop her, or I'll burn up on the spot.*

Like a father talking to a toddler, Marc waggled his finger in Linda's face. "Let's take it one step at a time, Linda. I'm sorry, but I don't even know who you are, so there's no way there's going to be an announcement of any engagement."

"But you promised, darling." Linda pulled on his arm. "On my birthday, you said."

Over Linda's shoulder, Marc's eyes sent an unspoken appeal to Jodie.

Jodie took a deep breath. "How about we all sit down, have our cups of tea, and sort out what's best for Joe, uh, Marc?"

Her brows knitting together, Linda pulled him down onto the couch with her and put her arm through his. Eve went to hand around the tea. Gently Marc extricated himself from Linda and stood up. "Let me do that for you, Mum." He handed Jodie a cup of tea.

"Thank you." She turned to his mother. "Eve, Joe's, uh, Marc's gear is out in the car. Is it okay if he stays here with you for the day and then tonight?"

Eve beamed. "Of course, where else?"

"He's got a specialist appointment tomorrow, so I'll come back and pick him up for that."

Linda put up her hand. "I could do that. I've got tomorrow off as well as today. Remember, Marc, I'm a nurse. I could be a great help to you."

Marc gulped. "Uh, it's all right, thanks, Linda. Jodie's still on holiday, so I'll go with her."

"But, darling…" Her face took on a hangdog look.

Marc shrugged and turned to his mother. "Until I can get my memory back, I'm really pretty useless."

Linda's face brightened. "I'll help you get it back, darling, you'll see."

The cuckoo jumped out of the cuckoo clock on the wall. "Cuck-oo, cuck-oo!"

Jodie's lips twisted. "Hey, is that the time? I'll have to run. Thanks for the tea and lovely shortbreads, Eve. Want to come and get your gear out of the car, Marc? Howzat, I got your name right at last."

He threw her a raspberry.

Linda jumped up and attached herself to his arm like a clamp. Her face wreathed in smiles, Eve walked beside them.

Jodie shook her head. *Boy, you're on your own now, Joe/Marc. Hope you survive the Clinging Vine and the Loving Mum.*

He closed her car door for her.

Your beseeching look would have made me laugh if I hadn't been so angry with Linda. She touched his hand on the window frame. "Good luck."

On and off all the way home, she chanted, "Marc, Marc, Marc."

Over dinner she shared her day's adventures with her parents and Tiffany. She pulled an exasperated face. "But I'm still struggling over Joe/Marc's name."

Chapter 8

The following morning Jodie knocked on Eve's front door. His facial hair trimmed neatly, Marc opened it.

Staring at him dressed in a white shirt and gray trousers and black jacket, Jodie giggled. "Wow, who is this? Mr. Sartorial Elegance himself? Maybe I can think of you as a Marc after all."

A woman's voice called from the top of the drive. "Hi, there." Jodie looked around and groaned. *Not the Clinging Vine again.*

Marc sighed. "Mum's gone off to her Clinic—she told me she's a receptionist for a dentist there. Linda's already come over once before to see if I needed anything."

Gritting her teeth, Jodie nodded. As Linda hurried toward them, Marc came out and locked the door behind him.

Linda pouted. "Marc won't let me come with him today. You'd think an engaged couple shouldn't be split at a time like this, wouldn't you?"

Both of them ignoring her remark, Marc followed Jodie to her car and they climbed in. Linda went to the passenger window and threw him a kiss. "See you, darling!

Jodie pulled out from the curb and Marc gave Linda a wave. "See you."

As they cruised along the main road, Jodie glanced over at her passenger. "Anything to report?"

"Not a thing. But I have taken to Mum okay."

"The old gut feeling at work again?"

"Uh huh. Hasn't let me down yet."

"Well, Eve's a real sweetie—you don't have to be psychic to appreciate what a nice person she is. What about your dad? Is he still around?"

"No, according to Mum, he died three years ago—cancer."

"I'm sorry."

"I would be too—if I could remember him. He obviously meant a lot to Mum."

She shook her head. "And what about the beautiful Linda?"

"Do I detect a note of sarcasm, or is it jealousy?"

"Whatever. Get on with it."

"There's not a thing—not a twinge. Not an anything."

"What about gut feeling?"

"Nothing." He looked shrewdly at Jodie. "So there's not a thing to be jealous about."

"You've got to give her a fair go."

"What do you mean?"

"Until you know the relationship you shared, you can't treat her like a new girl you've met."

"But she means nothing to me. For goodness sake, how do you suggest I treat her?"

Jodie shrugged. "That's up to you."

"Listen, all I feel like at the moment is getting you to pull up the car so I can cover you with kisses."

With a sideways look, Jodie gave him an arch smile.

"Instead, would you prefer I do that to Linda on the off-chance I was once really in love with her?"

A sharp knife turned inside her. "If you ever loved me, you could never have loved a girl like Linda—we're completely different types."

"Think I don't know that?" He rubbed a finger up her leg.

"Don't do that—I'm driving!"

****

When Marc came out of the specialist's, Jodie jumped up. "You're looking ultra-serious. Everything okay?"

"You're looking at Mr. Miracle Man. Apparently, I shouldn't be walking around like this—the blow was hard enough to have killed anyone with a skull of normal thickness."

Jodie flinched.

"The only reason I survived is because my skull is thicker than normal."

"Could the specialist tell what caused your injury?"

"Possibly a gun."

"My gosh!"

Near Eve's place, Jodie glanced over at Marc. "Joe, Marc, whatever you want to call yourself, I just want you to know I'm always here for you, but I won't be around for a while."

His head shot around. "Why not?"

"I go back to work tomorrow. If my boss likes my Broome collection, I'll have to work hard to put it together as a book. Meanwhile, you need to rebuild your relationships with your mum and Miss Clinging Vine. While all that's going on, there's no room for me anyway."

Marc said nothing.

A car was parked outside Eve's house. Jodie whistled. "Were you expecting visitors?"

Marc's fists clenched. "I've got a gut feeling about that car, but I don't know how to interpret it."

"Maybe you should sneak out with your plaster cast of that tire mark."

Marc's eyes narrowed.

Two burly men, one about forty and the other about fifty years of age, were sitting in the car. As Jodie turned and pulled up in the drive, the men got out. The smaller, older, and balder of the two men approached Marc. "Good afternoon, O'Connors. Remember me, your boss, Scott Masters?"

The younger man with a short back-and-sides haircut nodded to Marc.

His boss gave Marc a broad smile and stretched out his hand. Unsmiling, Marc shook it.

The second man clapped Marc on the upper arm and put out his hand. "Great to see you again too, Marc. I'm Rex Johns, your old partner."

Marc nodded and shook hands. He turned to Jodie. "This is my friend, Jodie."

She gave him a sharp look. *Did you omit to say my surname on purpose?*

The men nodded to her.

She nodded back. "Have you been here long?"

Scott glanced at his watch. "About ten minutes."

His eyes steely, Marc pointed to the house. "You'd better come inside. I guess we've got things to talk about."

Scott Masters laughed. "You're right about that!"

Jodie turned toward her car. "If you'll excuse me,

I'll be getting along."

Marc flashed her a look of urgent appeal. "Don't go, please, Jodie. Perhaps you wouldn't mind doing the traditional female thing and getting us all a cup of tea."

A voice called from the road. "Did I hear you mention a cup of tea? I can make you one."

Jodie's head whipped around. *Not you again, Linda. Serve you right if you get run over belting across the street without looking and listening in to other people's conversations.*

Marc's eyes blazed. "Uh, Linda, this is my boss, Scott Masters, and my partner, Rex Johns."

Johns shook hands. "Pleased to meet you, Linda."

"Pleased to meet you too. I'm Linda Amara— Marc's fiancée. I guess he's mentioned me to you lots of times."

Rex Johns frowned. "No, can't say I recall, but I take it you're the young lady who rang Scott to let us know Marc had returned."

Jodie's eyebrows nearly disappeared into her hairline. Marc's neck glowed red, and he glared at Linda. "Thanks for your offer, but this is police business. Please go back home."

Linda pouted and went to say something more, but Marc's glare intensified. He turned on his heel and followed Jodie to the house. Shoulders slumped, Linda watched the other two men join him.

When Jodie carried tea and biscuits into the lounge room, the three men looked up with serious expressions on their faces. She gave a forced smile. *Boy, you could cut the atmosphere in here with a meat cleaver.* Quickly she left the tray and retreated to the kitchen again.

Someone knocked on the back door and Jodie

peered out the window. Then she unlocked it. Linda walked in. "Only me."

Quickly Jodie stepped in front of her. "Sorry, Linda, Marc's busy. He's got a lot on his plate at the moment."

"I know. I'm only trying to be helpful. Poor Marc needs me more than ever now that he can't remember anything. If anyone can help him, it's me."

Jodie raised her eyebrows. "Why's that?"

"Because we love each other, and love is a pretty powerful tool."

Jodie exhaled audibly. The sound of a door closing came from the front of the house. Then came the sound of a car driving off. His face thunderous, Marc stormed into the kitchen, "How the hell did they know I was back and know all about my amnesia?" Catching sight of Linda, his face tightened. "What was that about your ringing them?"

"That's right, I rang them. Because I knew you were only half with it, I rang up and asked for your boss and told him the whole story. So I sort of knew Scott before you introduced us."

With a groan Marc sat down heavily. "Damn, I guessed from what was said earlier, it must have been something like that."

"Why, what's wrong with my calling them? You would have called them yourself if you'd thought of it. When they asked when they could see you, I even told them when you were likely to get back."

Clenching and unclenching his fists, Marc snapped, "Linda, do me a favor and butt out of my affairs. Please."

"But I'm your fiancée." Her lip trembled.

Jodie stared at her forlorn face. *Geez, I could almost feel sorry for you, you silly little moo.*

Marc banged his fist on the table. "Then take it the engagement's off!"

Linda cringed. "You can't mean that, Marc. You're not yourself!"

"The door." Marc pointed to the door. "Jodie will see you out."

Jodie gritted her teeth. *I'd prefer you kept me out of this, thanks.* But, looking again at his menacing expression, she took Linda's arm.

Linda snatched it away. "How come you get to stay here and I can't? I'm the one who's engaged to him."

"Take it easy, Linda, Marc's got his reasons for wanting to take things slowly. Don't rush him, or you won't get anywhere."

In a huff, Linda walked out the door and stomped off across the front lawn.

"Thank god that mad woman's gone!" Marc stopped pacing around the kitchen and pretended to tear his hair out. "That woman's had hallucinations—there's no way, not even if someone doped me up with cocaine, that I'd ever have got engaged to her. She might look all right, but as soon as she opens her mouth, my god!"

Poor Linda. No need to ever feel jealous of her. "How did you get on with Scott and Rex?"

"You're not very perceptive if you haven't noticed I'm in the biggest state of paranoia I've been in since you met me."

"Why?"

"Well, my gut feeling isn't working for Scott Masters—I don't know what I think about him. But that other guy—is he bad news! It took me all my time not to throw up all over him when he put out his hand for me to shake."

"You think he might have had something to do with your injury?"

"Absolutely. Masters told me he'd assigned Johns and me to investigate a drug case together. We'd followed leads to Port Hedland where we were supposed to have busted a couple of small-time smugglers with an Asian background. They were working for a Mr. Big from Broome." His brow furrowed. "Johns said we'd tracked the smugglers down and sprung them in a house at Port Hedland. But then two other druggies we didn't know about were supposed to have dashed into the room with guns and taken over. Johns said they'd slugged him, and when he'd come to, he'd found himself tied up, gagged, and locked in a cupboard. He reckoned it was hours before he managed to get free and get help. According to him, he had no idea what had happened to me. Although the local police and detectives they brought up from Perth searched for me, they found no sign of me, or of the smugglers."

"Did you believe him?"

"No way."

"Why not?"

"Apart from my gut feeling, the guy was just too on edge. If I'd said 'Boo,' I reckon he'd have pulled out his gun and started firing in any direction, especially mine."

"You think he'd have a vested interest in your not regaining your memory?"

A grim look on his face, Marc nodded.

"You reckon he could have a motive to make sure

you never regain it?"

"You can say that again."

"Well, where to from here?"

"I'm going to have to go into hiding."

"Isn't that taking your paranoia a bit far?"

"I thought you were on my side."

"I am." Jodie looked thoughtful. "If you reckon it's that serious, how about I provide you with a hiding place where no one should find you?"

A disbelieving look on his face, Marc stared at her. "Where?"

"When Tiff and I and our brother Kieran were kids, Dad and Mum bought a small holiday house down the coast a bit—near Rockingham. It takes less than an hour to drive there. How about I drive you there, drop you off and then return home alone? Interested?"

"Fine." Marc's eyes gleamed, and he squeezed her hands. "I'd prefer it if you stayed with me though."

While he threw some clothes into his pack, Jodie browsed through a photo album she found in the lounge room. A smiling baby with Marc's eyes and curls and then a young boy at various ages looked out at her. Her heart flipped.

"Ready?" Marc called softly as he came up behind her and planted a kiss on the back of her neck. He peered over her shoulder. "Don't tell me you're looking at my kid photos?"

"Sometimes you're earnest, sometimes laughing, but always you seem to be such an open sort of a kid. Yet here you are today with me knowing more about your early life than you do. It's weird."

He kissed the back of her neck again.

"I wish you wouldn't—you're supposed to be

engaged, remember?"

"Even someone knocked on the back of the head with a sledge-hammer would remember if he'd committed himself to a lifetime of bliss with the lovely Linda or not."

Jodie grinned and her heart beat faster.

Marc propped a note in front of a small vase of flowers in the middle of the table. "How's this sound? 'Had to go, Mum. Will be in touch. Love, Joe.' " He scratched out the *Joe* and substituted *Marc*.

With Marc at the wheel, Jodie rested back in the passenger seat and closed her eyes. "How do I do it? Now I'm on the run with a fugitive from someone or something."

Unsmiling, Marc glanced in the rear view mirror. "You know, I don't know much about what's going on, but I have the distinct feeling I'm not the most popular guy in certain quarters. If someone's really out to get me, it could put you in danger too."

A chill ran through her.

"I think we should plan some strategies for any eventuality."

Suddenly, the car shot forward. Jodie pushed her hands hard against the dashboard. "What's going on?"

"A white sedan's following us. Hang on while I see if I can lose him."

Jodie looked in the passenger outside mirror. A white sedan sat two cars behind them. A bearded man in dark glasses and wearing a beanie pulled down over his ears was hunched over the wheel, and another figure slouched down low in the passenger seat. Marc passed the few cars on the road with them, and the white sedan followed.

Traffic lights ahead turned amber. Marc accelerated across the intersection. The white sedan screeched to a stop. Marc exhaled. "Lucky for us a cop car was waiting to cross, or those hoods would be in our back seat with us right now."

As he passed several cars, Jodie held tight to her seat.

Marc glanced up a side street. "Any short cuts I can take away from the main roads."

"There's a park up the road a bit. Want to hide there?"

"Worth a try."

Marc swung the car off the road, drove down into the park and around a corner, and parked the far side of bushes in the empty car park. Quickly they jumped out.

The white sedan roared off the road and down the park toward them. Marc grabbed Jodie's hand and they ran along a path leading into dense bush.

The white sedan screeched to a halt. Two shots rang out. Belting single file through the undergrowth following Marc, Jodie sobbed. *My lungs are going to burst.* Moments later her feet started to bog down. *We're on a river bank!*

Floundering through reeds, she and Marc reached thigh-deep water. Both took enormous breaths and dived in.

Another shot rang out. Jodie swam underwater to the reeds on the far side of the river. Lungs close to bursting, she raised her nose to the surface. *Marc, where are you, Marc? Are you all right?*

Tears poured down her face. Concealed in the reeds, she pricked up her ears. *Someone's crashing and splashing about on the far side of the river. But I can't hear you, Marc. Where are you?* Keeping herself out of sight, she swam and pushed her way among the reeds looking for him.

A few minutes later another car entered the park. The crashing and splashing stopped, and soon after a car started up and drove off. Raising her head, Jodie listened intently. *That must be the thugs in the white sedan leaving the park.*

Quickly she swam into the open. "Marc, Marc!"

There was no answer.

About twenty meters downstream, she saw a large tree lying in the river. Trapped in its branches was something big. Jodie stroked faster. A body lay face down. "Marc!"

She reached him and turned his face up. *Oh, no, you're not breathing!*

Grabbing and holding his face steady, she breathed into his mouth and nose. Treading water, she performed the Kiss of Life a number of times. In between breaths, she tried to steer his body closer to the bank. Ringlets of red mixed with the water. Jodie's heart almost stopped. *No, no!*

She dragged Marc out of the river and continued to give him mouth-to-mouth resuscitation. After a few minutes, his chest rose and fell erratically.

"Oh, Marc, Marc!"

Marc coughed several times and opened his eyes. "Waz goin' on?"

"I've just brought you back from the dead, that's what's going on." Jodie covered his face with kisses. "Remember the guy in the white sedan fired shots at us and we took to the water? Later there was blood in the water. Where did he get you?"

Marc turned to look at the back of his left upper arm. "Check the top of this arm. It feels as though someone's shoved it with a red-hot poker." A scarlet stain was spreading on his shirt.

Jodie shivered. "Come on, it's time we got you to hospital."

Marc struggled upright and took a closer look at the wound on the back of his upper arm. "No, no hospitals. "Take me to your dad's surgery. He can patch me up."

Jodie pursed her lips. "Then we'd better move— the white sedan might come back."

"Okay, you're the boss." Marc tried to lift himself to his feet and winced.

With Jodie taking some of his weight, they stumbled along a bush track parallel to the water. It led to a narrow footbridge across the river.

Back at the car, Jodie settled Marc into the passenger seat and grabbed a wad of tissues from the glovebox. She held them against his wound. "Hold your arm up and press the tissues against your wound to stop losing any more blood."

She glanced around. Two more cars had pulled in beside her car. Quickly she walked around to the driver's side of the car. *What a sight I must look.* A man and woman from the car two up looked her way and their mouths fell open. Jodie forced a cheery smile. "Got a bit close to the river bank and fell in."

She snapped on her seatbelt and turned the heater on full blast. "Marc, Mr. White Sedan's sure to be hanging around up top somewhere, so slide down so he can't see you. Then he won't know whether to follow me or to come back here looking for you."

As they were driving toward the exit, Jodie went white. "The sedan's blocking the exit."

"Go out the entrance!"

Jodie did a smart U-turn and drove back down the semi-circular track and out the entrance. "Keep down! The sedan's waiting for us." She gripped the wheel hard. "I'll take some side streets and give them the slip."

Her knuckles white, she accelerated past several cars. The traffic lights ahead shone red. She braked. "Mr. White Sedan's only three cars behind. Want me to drive to the nearest police station?"

"No, I don't know which police I can trust."

The traffic lights changed. Jodie zoomed off. At the first side street, she whipped off the main road, and the white sedan followed. She tore around corner after corner. By the time she had taken ten quick turns, she was back on the major road heading for her father's surgery.

For the twentieth time she checked her rear vision mirror. "No sign of Mr. White Sedan for five turns now, Marc. Give it a bit longer and you can come up."

Several kilometers down the road, she patted his arm. "Looks like we've lost him for good. Like to come up now? How's the crook arm?"

"As good as I'd imagine anyone in soaking wet clothes scrunched up on the floor of a car and with a piece of his flesh with a hole blasted through it feels." He gritted his teeth and sat up in the passenger seat. He flexed the fingers of his right hand and again pressed hard on the blood-soaked tissues against his wound.

Jodie bit her lip. "Do you reckon it will be safer to take you to my place and wait for Dad or go to Dad's surgery?"

"The surgery. I'm losing too much blood to wait."

Increasing her speed, Jodie hit an intersection as the lights turned amber. She accelerated harder. "Sorry, this is becoming a bit of a habit."

As she approached her father's surgery, she glanced in her rear vision mirror. She gave a low whistle. "Still no sign of Mr. White Sedan."

In the car park she helped Marc out of the car and sneaked him and his backpack through a back door into the tea room. "Guess it's something we've both dried out a bit and we're not dripping anymore."

From Marc's backpack she took out a tee shirt and a pair of jeans and handed them to him. Then she waved some underpants. "I guess you need these too."

He reddened. "Sorry, but I don't think I'll be able to manage to get into those by myself."

Stifling giggles and adopting a sober expression, Jodie helped him get out of his wet clothes and into dry ones.

Then she peered into the backpack again. "I hope you've got something in here that fits me too."

Dressed in an over-sized tee shirt and shorts, she giggled. "Hope none of Dad's patients or staff sees me."

Between patients, Jodie sneaked into her father's surgery. As she explained the situation to him, his face became more and more concerned. Quickly he came and lay Marc down in a vacant surgery and staunched the blood coming from his arm. After seeing his last patients for the day and sending his receptionist home early, Tom quickly returned to Marc and probed around his arm. Marc winced.

"Hmm, lucky it's only a flesh wound, but you will have to be careful of infection."

Before long the bullet was out and lying in a stainless-steel dish. "I guess you want me to keep this until it's needed as evidence sometime against your Mr. White Sedan?"

His patient nodded. "Getting around in Jodie's car will be a problem though. Whoever's after me knows it now. If police are out to get me, it won't take much for Mr. White Sedan to ring around and let his cronies know to look out for me. They're also sure to have checked off the registration and come up with Jodie's name and address by now anyway."

Tom breathed out heavily. "You really should get onto the police and get yourself police protection."

"What if they assign Rex Johns or Mr. White Sedan as my bodyguard? I'm sorry, Tom, until I get my memory back, I'm really not in a position to know which police to trust."

"I don't want to make this any harder for you, Marc, but I also have to worry about Jodie's safety. It could have been her and not you who collected that bullet today."

Eyes fiery, Jodie glared at her father. "That's not fair, Dad. I knew there were risks and I took them."

Marc's mouth twisted. "Your dad's right. I'm sorry you've had to get involved. If I can just get to your holiday house and lie low until this arm heals, I'll be out of your hair."

Tom handed Jodie his key pouch. "That's the key to my car."

Jodie's mouth fell open.

"You've got more chance of getting down to

Rockingham in my car without being seen and followed."

"But what about you? You'll be in danger too if you take my car."

"It can stay here, and I'll get a lift or a taxi home and use Mum's car until you get back with mine."

Jodie threw her arms around her father. "Oh, Dad, thank you." She frowned. "But what about my car being a bit damp from us being in the river? Not to mention a bit of blood."

Without saying a word, Tom pointed to the door.

Marc lay on the back seat, and Jodie drove out onto the street. She exhaled audibly. "Gee, I've only driven Dad's car a couple of times before. It's much harder to maneuver." She glanced both ways. "All clear, thank goodness."

****

At a small elevated, fibro-cement holiday house opposite the foreshore, Jodie pulled up, opened Marc's door, and helped him out. "Welcome to the Winters' Rockingham residence."

She unlocked the front door and gave Marc her shoulder to lean on. As he climbed the stairs inside, sweat gathered on his forehead. At the top of the stairs, Jodie switched on a light, and they stepped into a large L-shaped rectangular living-room with a kitchen up the far end.

She walked across the room to full-length gold drapes. "Take a look at this." She pulled the curtains open and revealed French doors opening onto a balcony. "From up here, you'll have a bird's eye view of anyone who arrives. Not to mention glimpses of the sea."

She walked over to a small room opposite the kitchen area. "This is Kieran's old room. You'll be comfortable in here. Tiff's and my room is next to it. The master bedroom's next to the kitchen area."

****

In the early morning, Jodie peeped into Marc's room and smiled. "Sleeping like the sweetest baby."

Later as she changed his dressing, he winced.

"Sorry, I'm not the gentlest nurse."

With Marc sleeping most of the Saturday away, Jodie busied herself spring-cleaning. A window with salt-embedded crust resisted her scrubbing. *I don't know when these windows last had a wash.*

During the afternoon, Jodie looked in the cupboards. *Hmm, Mum always keeps a decent lot of groceries for meals down here. Pity we didn't have a chance to pick up some fresh meat, fruit, and veggies though. I could have made a decent stew for us and made enough for several more meals for Marc.*

For dinner she opened a tin of mushroom soup, one of peas, and one of tuna and heated them in a pot on the small gas stove. In another pot she boiled brown rice.

Marc ate the serving of tuna casserole Jodie gave him. "Hmm, very tasty, thanks."

"Good. With a bit of luck, you'll get another two or three meals out of this."

****

On Sunday morning, Jodie tapped on Marc's door and walked in. His eyes closed, he lay still. She leaned over and listened to his rhythmic breathing. "You're a bit of a boring companion. You've hardly said 'boo' to me in the day and two nights I've been here."

"Boo!" Marc opened his eyes and grabbed her with

his good arm, pulling her down onto his bed.

"Not fair, not fair." Jodie pulled herself up and softly kissed his mouth.

He allowed Jodie to help him dress and sat at the table with her to have breakfast. "Tell me about your holidays here when you were a kid."

Between sleeps on the couch and watching the news on the old television in the sitting room, Marc spent the day talking to Jodie and hearing about her life in Perth and holidays at Rockingham.

A morose look crossed his face. "I wish I could remember stuff like that about my early life."

Jodie squeezed his hand. "At least now you've got your mum and your photo albums to tell you about it."

****

"Take care, Jodie." Marc kissed her. "I wish you didn't have to return to work today."

She buried her face in his chest, "Oh, Marc, I hate having to go. I don't want to leave you here alone."

"I'll be fine. There's lots of tinned and packet food in the cupboards. You just go home and return your dad's car with my thanks. Then go to work and wow them with your Broome paintings and sketches."

"Do you reckon it'll be safe for me to come back on Friday night and spend the weekend with you?"

"Probably not, but if you don't come, I'll die anyway. See if you can borrow your dad's car again."

Chapter 9

"Not bad, not bad at all," Kenny murmured, his eyes carefully assessing each of Jodie's Broome paintings. "You're going to be a busy person getting these all put together over the next few weeks."

Jodie glowed like the coals of a long-burning fire. *Coming from you, Kenny, that's full-on praise.*

At ten o'clock the phone rang. "Hello, Jodie, it's Eve. I hope you don't mind but I got your mother to give me your work number. Do you know where Marc is? I've been worried sick about him."

Turning her head, Jodie lowered her voice. "No need to worry, Eve. Sorry I can't talk now. Any chance you can come to town and meet me for lunch one day this week?"

****

That day, the two met at a small cafe near Jodie's work. Throwing her arms around the younger woman, Eve hugged her tight. Over their meal, Jodie told Eve what had happened, but gave no details as to Marc's whereabouts. "It's for his protection—and yours, and, please, not a word to anyone."

"What about Linda? Being his fiancée, she's got a right to know, hasn't she?"

"I'm sorry, Eve, and especially not Linda. She's the reason Marc's on the run."

"What do you mean?"

Jodie gave an edited version of the situation.

At the end of it, Eve groaned. "Poor Marc, and poor Linda, she can be so indiscreet. It's not the first time she's landed herself in hot water, and it's usually been good old Marc who's had to get her out. He even had to be her deb partner after she went and told everyone she had a partner and she didn't."

"Oh."

"You've no idea what a surprise their engagement was. Linda's a lovely girl with a heart of gold, and I love her dearly. But Marc never showed the slightest interest in her other than that of a big brother."

Oh, Eve, that's so good to know—especially coming from you.

"When Marc's father died of cancer, she was an absolute pillar of strength to me. Because Brian wanted to die at home, she offered to come over to our place to help nurse him. She couldn't have done more for us, and we're very grateful to her."

Jodie nodded. *Explains a lot.* She gave herself a shake. *Come on, be charitable.*

****

As the weekend got closer, Jodie started to have butterflies in her stomach. *Oh, Marc, I can't wait to see you again.* On the Friday she caught the bus home.

As she loaded her father's car with her overnight bag and car fridges containing the fresh bread, milk, meat, fruit, and vegetables her mother had bought for her that day, Tom joined her. "Keep your eyes peeled all the time, Jodie. If you suspect you're being followed and you can't shake whoever it is off, head for the nearest police station or come back here."

"Got it, Commissioner. Now any orders for your

patient?"

"Well, I hope he was able to change his dressings without help. Make sure when you do the job, there's no sign of infection."

As Jodie turned out of her street, a small black hatchback parked on the far side of the road started up and put on its flick light. Jodie gulped. *Uh, oh, that's not a car I remember seeing before, and I can't see who's in it.*

Driving through a well-lit shopping center several kilometers on, she checked her rear-vision mirror. The small black hatchback was close behind. Jodie let out a whistle. Pulling over, she watched the car go past. A balding blond man in his early thirties was driving it. Suddenly, his car's left-hand indicator flicked and he went to pull in fifty meters ahead of her. Adrenalin rushed through Jodie. "Time for evasive action, and don't panic."

She pulled back into the traffic. The blond man immediately pulled out after her. Accelerating along the road, she passed the car in front of her. *Good, there's no room for the blond man to follow.*

Once past several more cars, she quickly turned off onto a side street. She stepped on the accelerator and tore along the street, whipped around a corner, and then another and another. A few more turns on, she turned into a major street running parallel with the one she had started in. She glanced in the rear vision mirror. No other car was in sight. She exhaled deeply.

Some time later, Jodie hit the coast road. She took in a deep breath, and then slowly let it out. *It is so good to feel free again; I feel like an eagle must feel catching a thermal.*

At the holiday house, the curtains were drawn. Jodie frowned. Quickly she unlocked the downstairs door, went in, locked the door behind her, and ran up the inside stairs to the living-room. "Marc!" she called. "Marc, I'm back!"

Upstairs was in pitch blackness. Jodie's body tensed. Leaving on the lights over the stairs, she turned on the lights in the living room. Warily she walked in. "Marc, are you there, Marc?"

The hairs on the back of her neck stood up. She put down her overnight bag and handbag and stared into the blackness. "Marc, it's me, Jodie."

She walked to a small table nearby and picked up an empty vase. Gripping it firmly, she slowly pushed open Marc's bedroom door and switched on his light. "Marc...?" Her voice stuck in her throat—his bed was empty though slept in.

At a sudden movement from behind the door Jodie went to spin around. A heavy weight threw itself on her and smashed her front first onto the bed. Someone forced her right arm up behind her back. She cried out and the vase dropped from her right hand and tumbled onto the bed.

"Who are you and what are you doing here?"

The rough male voice chilled her. "Let me go!"

The man forced Jodie's arm farther up her back. "Tell me who you are and what you are doing here."

Pain shot up her arm. "I'm Jodie, and this is my parents' house."

The man pushed harder against her arm.

"Stop or you'll break my arm!"

The weight was lifted off her back.

As Jodie slowly turned, rubbing her arm, her heart

almost stopped. Dressed in his pajamas and with the vase held in position ready to strike, Marc stood menacingly above her. Her eyes widened. "Marc, what's wrong?"

"Shut up. I'll ask the questions."

Tight-faced, Jodie sat on the edge of the bed and clamped her lips together.

"What am I doing here?"

Her brow furrowed. "You don't remember?"

"Stop playing games." Marc held the vase closer to her face.

"It's me—Jodie. You must remember me. We...I—" Jodie broke off as hard, cold eyes raked her face.

"How long have I been a prisoner here?"

"You're not a prisoner. I brought you here to recover from your bullet wound, remember? You've been here since last Friday night."

"Who shot me? You?"

"No, no." Involuntary tears trickled down her cheeks. "The man who was following us in the white sedan shot at both of us when we were in the river. Don't you remember?"

His expression hardened.

Jodie jumped up. "You haven't had a fall, have you?" As she went to touch the back of his head, Marc dropped the vase and grabbed her hand in a vice-like grip.

"You give me any trouble and you'll regret it."

"You must trust me. I'd never hurt you. What's the last thing you remember? Do you remember being in Broome?"

He looked blankly at her.

"What about Port Hedland? Do you remember going to Port Hedland with Rex Johns?"

He forced Jodie back onto the bed. "How do you know about that?"

"You told me. Over two months ago, you were hit on the head and you lost your memory. Do you remember who hit you on the head?"

His eyes narrowed. "Yes, that lying crook, Johns."

"That's wonderful—you have got your memory back after all." Jodie jumped up and went to throw her arms around his neck, but he pushed her back on the bed. Her mouth puckered. "You don't remember me at all, do you?"

His expression as hostile as ever, Marc stood over her, his body poised like a warrior's ready to strike. "I think you've got a lot of talking to do, Jodie, or whatever your real name is."

She licked her dry lips. "Yes, but you're a sick man—you should be in bed. How about you get into bed and I'll come and sit beside you?"

Though he looked as if he were going to refuse, the lines beside his mouth were deepening. "Prove to me who you are first."

"I've got my license in my bag. Will that do? I've also got a pile of food for you in my dad's car in the carport under the house."

Marc examined her license. Without a word, he pulled a jacket around his shoulders with his good hand and arm. "Now, let's have a look in your car."

He followed her downstairs. Like a criminal in a B-grade movie, he looked about before going to the car.

From the boot, Jodie took out two car fridges and several loaded plastic bags of groceries. Marc put out his hand for the bigger car fridge. Jodie let out a sigh of relief. *Well, that's an improvement.*

Back in the living-room, Jodie peered at his face. "You've gone quite gray. Please get back into bed."

His eyes slowly closing and opening, he did so.

"Time for hot chocolate. Give me a couple of minutes, and I'll make us both one."

When she carried the drinks in, Marc was lying in bed with his eyes closed. She pulled a chair up next to him. His face drawn, he turned to face her. Then she gave him a brief rundown of events involving him over the previous couple of months as she knew them.

"Sounds like you've been a good friend to me. I don't know why you bother—I've been such a bear to you."

Jodie shrugged. "There's a lot more, but it can wait until later."

"What about my mother? You reckon she's not too worried about my disappearance?"

"She's worried all right, but not half as worried as she would have been if she hadn't caught up with what was going on last Monday. Because I couldn't tell her anything over the phone, she met me for lunch."

Slipping farther down under the bedclothes, Marc winced. Jodie leaned forward. "Hey, how's the top of your arm? Dad gave me express instructions to change the dressing as soon as I got here. I have to check there's no infection."

After washing her hands and preparing the new dressing, Jodie took off the old one. "Hmm."

"Hmm what?"

"Looks pretty good to me. There's no sign of infection—it's just a bit red, though that could be caused by your attack on me."

"What attack? I never touched you."

Jodie rolled her eyes and then looked closely at his tight face. "You don't look so good though."

"What's wrong with me?"

"Your face is gray, and it's tight. Have you been taking your antibiotics?"

"I guess so. When I went exploring this morning, I saw a bottle out in the kitchen. It wasn't full so I guessed they were for me. I haven't taken any today though."

"Right, as soon as I clean you up and put on a fresh dressing, I'll get a capsule for you. You can't afford to get septicemia or something." Like a skilled professional, Jodie replaced the dressing.

Then she took a capsule from the bottle in the kitchen and handed it to Marc. "Take this."

"How do I know it's not a cyanide capsule?"

"You don't. You'll just have to trust me, won't you?"

Unsmiling, he took the capsule, put it in his mouth and swallowed it down with a mouthful of water.

"Okay, now you've heard what I know, it's time for you to tell me what you know. How does all that I've told you fit in with what you know and remember?"

"I can remember everything up to when someone slammed down a gun on my head. It had to have been Rex Johns. If it had been anyone else, Johns would have had time to warn me."

"When he came around to your mum's to see you, you said you had a gut feeling about him, so it looks as though your gut feeling was right. What about your boss—Scott Masters?"

Marc's brow furrowed. "I don't remember anything about him coming to my mum's. I can't remember anything from when Rex Johns brained me to my waking up here."

Tears filled Jodie's eyes, and she blinked them away.

"No idea about Scott Masters though. He could jump either way for all I know."

"What about Linda?"

"Linda, what about her?"

"Are you engaged to her?"

"Hell no. Whatever gave you that idea?"

Her heart gave a leap. "Nothing. Tell me, exactly when did you recover your old memory and lose your memory of incidents over the last two months or so?"

Marc frowned. "This morning, I guess."

"Any reason? Did you just wake up and think it was a couple of months ago, or did you have a fall or something?"

"I'm not sure exactly…. I remember having a terrible nightmare. It was so real, I thought it was actually happening." His eyes focused on a far wall as though he were reliving it.

"What was happening?"

"I was in the middle of a drug bust and Rex Johns was my back-up. Suddenly, I sensed a movement from behind me where he was. Before I could get more than a flash, I was brained with something heavy." He paused again.

"And?"

"I think I must have started screaming and throwing myself about. I must have fallen out of bed and maybe I did hit my head, or maybe I landed on my crook arm and the pain was so great I passed out. When I came to, I was lying on the floor half-frozen to death. Since I had no idea where I was, I went exploring. But, after a minute or two, I felt so cold and crook I had to crawl back into bed."

"Let's have a look at your head."

Marc turned his head and Jodie parted his hair. Gently she felt for a lump.

"Well, I can feel the big lump you brought with you from Broome, but there doesn't seem to be a second one."

"Great."

"Not great at all. You obviously have a problem, so must have done some damage. Are you sure you haven't got a death wish?"

He gave her a baleful look.

"I think you need a doctor to look at you again."

He glared. "No more doctors. Too dangerous."

Then he stroked the heavy stubble on his face. "Where did this come from?" He ran his hand down his curly hair. "And this?"

Alone in her room, Jodie prepared for bed. *I wish my head would stop racing. There's too much going on for me to take in.* She sighed. *I wish you were here to check your patient over, Dad.*

Chapter 10

Jodie knocked on Marc's door.

"Come in."

"You've lost that gray color you had. How are you feeling?"

"Apart from the arm that's been kicked by a mule and the head that's been stomped on, you mean?"

"I mean, it's a lovely day—the sun is shining and 'all's right with the world'. If you feel up to it, we could try a short walk along the beach. It's a pretty private beach at this time of the day and year—we probably won't meet anyone else at all."

His face darkened.

"That's if you don't think the risk is too great."

Slowly they walked along the beach together. Jodie sneaked a look at the surly-faced young man beside her. *If you were the old Marc, I'd grab your hand and race along the sand with you. But, boy, not you.*

Marc kicked at a piece of seaweed. "What are you thinking?"

"That it's nice not to be looking over my shoulder all the time."

"Yeah… But very soon someone else sure as hell will have to if he doesn't want to collect what he had in mind for me."

Jodie blanched. *You're using that threatening voice you used when you attacked me last night. What's happened to the gentle Joe and the attractive Marc guy you used to be?* She took a deep breath. "What do you mean?"

"It's either me or it's Rex Johns and his druggie boys."

"You can't mean you're going to…?"

"Don't look so worried—I'm not going to dispose of them, if that's what you're scared of. 'Course they'd be no loss if I did—the world would be a better place without them. I just mean I'm going to put them behind bars for a long time. C'mon, let's forget about them and enjoy the day."

Jodie reached out and touched him lightly on the arm. "Do you trust me?"

He turned, looked her in the eyes, and then slid his gaze away. Shrugging, he walked off.

Blinking away tears, she dragged along behind him. *How could you turn away like that? After all we meant to each other. How can I ever believe in you again?*

In a sheltered spot between sand dunes, Marc put his cap down and lay face down on it and closed his eyes. A short distance away, Jodie lay down on her back and covered her face with her arm. *At least the early morning sun is warm and loving.*

Several minutes later, Marc propped himself up on his good arm and stared into Jodie's face. The hair on her neck prickling, she opened her eyes. "What's up? Why the frown? Have I got raspberry jam smeared on my nose or something?"

"No, I was wondering what it would be like to kiss you."

"You already know." Jodie jumped to her feet and

took off the way they had come.

Marc ran and caught up to her. "Was there more to our relationship than just friendship?"

"Forget it. If you can't remember, it means nothing."

He stretched out his step to match hers. "Tell me about your life."

"I've already told you. Seeing you remember it now, it's your turn to tell me about yours."

"I'll tell you whatever you want to know. But if I'm to survive and possibly you too, it's essential I know what's going on and what's been going on. The thugs who are after me aren't likely to lie low for long."

Like a reluctant child pressured to divulge her secrets, Jodie told Marc more about her job, where she worked, about her parents and Tiffany, and about his mother and Linda.

He snorted. "You reckon Linda thinks she and I are engaged?"

"That's what she keeps saying."

"What an imagination she's got. Honestly, she was the kid sister I didn't have, and I was the big brother she didn't have, but that's as far as it ever went. I didn't think she'd ever read more into our friendship than there was."

"The minx. She's taken advantage of the situation or she's so infatuated with the idea of being in love she's created a giant fantasy in her mind and come to believe it's true."

He frowned. "She's not a bad kid. It's more likely the fantasy. But either way she's a problem I can do without."

Jodie glanced at Marc's profile, and her heart

skipped inside her. *Gee, won't I ever learn? Here I am falling in love with you all over again. But it's tough being in love with an enigma. It's as though you've got three different personalities—the Joe, the Marc 1, and the Marc 2. All your personalities and looks are a bit different but I love them all.* A picture of the aggressive side of Marc 2 flashed into her mind, and she shuddered. *No, not you.*

That afternoon, Marc lay on the couch reading the paper while Jodie sprawled on a beanbag in front of the French windows. With the sun streaming in, she dozed off and her magazine dropped from her hand.

Some time later, she woke. She looked up at Marc studying her features. Quickly she sat up and pulled her tee shirt straight. "What's up?"

"I'm just trying to remember you from before— I've got a good gut feeling about you, you know."

"Thanks, but you didn't give that impression last night."

He smiled and her heart flipped.

"Want to know what I thought when I had you lying on the bed looking up at me?"

Holding her breath, Jodie nodded.

"I thought you were the most beautiful girl I'd ever seen and I hoped like crazy you were nothing to do with the drug bust."

Her nerve endings pulsated crazily. "And…now…what do you think?"

"I still think and hope the same."

She took a deep breath and exhaled. "What do I have to do to prove to you that you can trust me?"

"Do you mind if I kiss you?"

Before she could answer, Marc was kneeling over

her and bringing his face toward hers and leaning her back against the beanbag. She tingled inside, and her mouth softened as his lips gently covered her own. *It is so good to feel you so close again, Marc. I can nearly weep with the joy of it.*

After long moments, he straightened up. With his good hand, he pulled her to her feet. Then he put his good arm around her and pressed her body against his and kissed her again. He pulled her toward the couch and sat her down. Then he sat next to her, put his arm around her shoulder and pulled her close again. "Were we ever lovers?"

Coloring Jodie looked down at her hands in her lap. "No." *But I'm not telling you the intimacies we shared.*

His eyes searched her face. "That's not the whole story, is it?"

She shook her head. "No, but you'll have to remember the rest because I'm not telling you."

"Did I touch you like this?" He ran his hand down her side. She froze. "And like this?" He cupped his hand around her breast.

Letting out a cry, Jodie sprang up and ran into her room. She slammed the door and pressed her back against it. Tears poured down her face. *How could he? He's just using me because he knows I care.*

There was a light knock on her door. "Jodie, I'm sorry, I didn't mean anything bad. Please come out—I promise I won't upset you again."

"Go away."

"Please, come out and talk to me."

A few minutes later a wary, red-eyed Jodie emerged from her bedroom. "What do you want to talk about?"

"I just want to tell you that I've never gone on like that before with a girl—I was acting completely out of character, and I'm sorry."

"Well, I've never gone on like that with a guy before. In fact…"

"Yes?"

"In fact, you're the first person I've ever shared a passionate kiss with."

"Oh, Jodie, you really are an old-fashioned girl, aren't you?"

"I know and the boys don't like it. Well, stiff cheese."

"I like it—I think it's great."

"Well, it doesn't get me anywhere."

"Would it surprise you to know I haven't exactly had what you'd call a mountain of experience where girls are concerned?"

Jodie's heart leapt inside her. "You haven't?"

"No, apart from anything else, I've been too busy with my career. The hours and the risky environment I move in don't exactly make dating girls easy. Yet, when I met you yesterday, I had a gut feeling I was missing out on something good. Tell me about our relationship…please."

"No, if you can't remember what we had, then we'll have to start from scratch."

His mouth drooped.

"Maybe we'll work up to what we had before, maybe not. Come on, do you play cards? There's a pack in the cupboard."

"Sure I play…although I can't see a one-handed card-player being much of an asset."

"Blow. How about a board game or something else then?"

****

On Sunday evening Jodie studied Marc as he watched the news on TV. *Engrossed as ever in anything to do with the police.* Like an indulgent mum, she smiled. *I reckon I now know Marc 2 as well as I know Joe and Marc.*

As he changed channels, she snuggled into his side. He smiled down at her. "Am I allowed to kiss your forehead?"

"Gee, I wish you'd get your act together and synthesize your three personalities, Marc."

At the end of the show they were watching, he turned to her. "I've decided to go back to Perth with you tomorrow."

"No. I thought you were going to stay in hiding for at least another week to get your strength back before you take on Rex Johns and his cronies."

"I've changed my mind. My arm feels so much better now and the headaches seem to be finished. If I don't get out and sort out Rex Johns, he might get a lucky break and start sorting me out."

"How? I told you how good I am at losing tails."

"Don't get too cocky. How do you know they haven't put a bug in the car or tapped your phone or your house or my mum's phone or house?"

"No!" Her mind raced. "But I've been so careful about what I say and where I say it. Why do you think I asked your mother to meet me in town for lunch? I do have a few brains."

"Keep your hair on. All I'm trying to do is to get you to realize you're not playing a board game here.

These guys know all the tricks, and the stakes are so high they play for keeps."

A shiver rippled through her body, and his arm tightened about her shoulders. "Then why go back into the lions' den where there's no one you can trust?"

"Oh, there are guys there I can trust. I just don't know about my boss. But I do know about my sidekick, Barney Baker. He's someone I can confide in and who can help me get to the bottom of it all."

Jodie's mouth quivered. "If you come back with me tomorrow, you've got to promise me you'll let Dad look you over."

Marc looked into her eyes. "I promise—but only after I sort out which guys I can trust to watch my back."

****

The following morning, it was dark when they left the house. Noiselessly, they clambered into the car. Marc reached across, patted Jodie's knee, and winked. She swallowed hard, smiled, and patted his knee back.

They drove in silence until the day dawned. As the sun peeped over the top of a hill and peppered the sky with gold all around, she broke into a song about the beauties of the morning.

Marc smiled and nodded.

It's so lovely to be able to express how I'm feeling without giving away Marc's presence if someone has planted a bug in the car.

An hour or so later, as pre-arranged, Jodie pulled up at police headquarters. She walked with Marc to the building. "Promise me you won't take any unnecessary risks."

He took her hands in his and kissed her lightly.

123

"Will do. With Barney's help, I'll get it worked out." He kissed her again. "Thanks for everything. Keep safe." Then he turned and disappeared into the building.

Jodie drove off. *I hope you're right about this Barney Baker, and he's as trustworthy as you think he is. How do you know he's okay, yet you don't know about Scott Masters? Surely such a pleasant guy as he seems to be couldn't be involved in heroin smuggling.* Her mouth drooped.

Back home, Jodie took her parents out into the back garden and, in a low voice, confided to them what had happened. The expression on their faces mirrored her own.

Tom shook his head. "Why didn't you bring Marc straight to me, Jodie? He needs to be looked over as soon as possible."

Chapter 11

Jodie stared out the window. *Why haven't you been in contact, Marc? It's been a full day and a night, and my nerves are stretched to breaking point.*

As she left work late the following afternoon, a figure stepped out of the shadows and dropped into step beside her. "Marc!" She threw her arms around him.

"Whoa." He gave her a quick peck. "Sorry, but we'll have to save that until later. Business first."

"Is it safe for you to be here?"

"Probably not, but I had to talk to you. I've got Barney with me as back-up if Rex Johns or his boys try anything."

Quickly she looked around.

"You didn't see anyone, did you?"

"No. Should I have?"

"No, but it shows you how good a professional Barney is. Don't look now, but take a look at the car parked behind yours."

Taking Marc's arm, Jodie half-turned him, looked up into his face, and then casually looked over his shoulder. "I can see a man in the car reading a newspaper, but he seems completely oblivious of us."

"He's listening to every word we're saying through a device I've got fitted in my top pocket."

"You haven't."

"It's okay—I've just turned it off."

Marc took his hand out of his pocket, and she grinned her relief.

"Quick, tell me what's going on."

"Rex Johns and Scott Masters think I'm reporting back on duty after regaining my memory except for the day of the drug-bust and the run-up to it. Everyone else at work except Barney thinks the same. We're working on leads to implicate Rex Johns with the two Asian guys I busted in Port Hedland."

"Were you able to get anywhere with the plaster cast you had of the tire mark you found?"

Marc's eyes narrowed. "Barney got a trusted analyst to identify the brand and the size of the tires for us. The analyst also told him the make of the vehicles using those tires."

She licked her lips. "Was it a match with the sort of tire to fit a car Rex Johns could have been driving?"

Eyes steely, he nodded. "It matched with the make of the unmarked police car he was driving. But the print wasn't good enough to identify a specific vehicle."

Jodie gripped his hand hard. "Promise me you'll be careful, Marc."

She walked to her car and unlocked it, and Marc climbed into the car behind and sat beside the man with the newspaper. As they drove off, Jodie looked at the man driving. Her heart went cold. *My god, Barney's the balding blond man in the black car who followed me the night I went to Rockingham.*

"Oh, Marc, your gut feeling has let you down terribly. How can I warn you?"

That night Jodie thrashed about and got little sleep. In the morning, Eve rang and arranged to meet her for lunch.

In a small café, Jodie told her all that had been going on with Marc since they had last met. Eve looked thoughtful. "This balding blond man you're talking about, his name's not Barney Baker, is it?"

"Yes, why?"

"Fantastic, because if it's Barney, we don't need to worry. Several years ago Marc saved his life, and there's no way he would ever let anyone hurt Marc."

Jodie snorted. "Why did he follow me then?"

"I don't know.... Perhaps he was watching you in the hope you'd lead him to Marc."

"That's what I've been trying to say all along."

"No, I don't mean for bad reasons—I mean, maybe he wanted to get to him to help him or to warn him or something."

"If he did, why didn't he tell Marc, and why didn't Marc tell me?"

"Perhaps he did, and Marc didn't think to tell you."

"Gee, what a mess."

During the day, Jodie heard nothing from Marc. Sighing, she turned into her drive that evening. A strange car was parked out the front of her house. She frowned.

As she let herself in the front door, Tiffany came running up. "Guess who's here."

Her body tingled. "Marc?"

A smiling, tanned young man followed Tiffany up the passage and enveloped her in a bear hug. "Oh, Ryan, when did you get back to Perth?"

"A couple of hours ago. Just had time to say hello to my folks, clean up, and get out here to see how Tiff was doing without me." He put his arm around Tiffany and pressed her close to his side.

Eyes shining, Tiffany looked up into his face. "Isn't it marvelous? I wasn't expecting him until the weekend at the earliest."

As the two talked away at dinner, Jodie smiled. *Lovely you're so happy to be together again. Even better if Marc was here too.*

Ryan turned to her. "What happened to Joe? Do you still keep in touch?"

She gave him a sickly grin.

"He was pretty taken with you, you know—if you'd only have given him the go-ahead, I reckon he'd have been yours for life."

Tom put up his hand. "Ryan, things are a bit delicate at the moment. Tiff can fill you in later."

Jodie gave her father a tremulous smile.

Ryan raised his eyebrows at Tiffany, and she squeezed his arm. "Yes, it's a long story. Come on, tell us some more about your travels."

Jodie rubbed her forehead. She turned to her sister, whose arm was intertwined with Ryan's. *Tiff, for your sake, I truly am pleased Ryan's here. But please get him to go home, so I can take Mum and Dad out into the garden to discuss my doubts about Barney.*

****

On her way to work the following day, Jodie dropped her car off for a major service. Tiffany followed her to the garage in their mother's car and then drove her to work. "'Bye, Jodie. Don't forget Ryan and I are picking you up this afternoon."

Every time the phone rang, Jodie rushed to pick up the receiver.

At lunchtime, she clenched her fists together. *If Marc doesn't ring today, or tomorrow morning at the latest, I'm going to do what Dad said to do. I'll go to police headquarters and demand to see the commissioner.*

Late that afternoon, Jodie headed out to the carpark near her work and looked around. She pulled a face. *Come on, Tiff and Ryan.*

A car in the car park started up and drove over to where Jodie was standing. The door opened and a slim man of Asian appearance and a bearded stocky man of European appearance jumped out. They grabbed her and bundled her into the back seat of their car. The European man rammed something hard and metallic into her side. "One squeak, sweetheart, and it will be your last."

Jodie whipped her head around. *Is that Mum's car turning into the carpark? Did Tiffany and Ryan see what happened?*

Her captor slammed her head down onto the seat. "Lie down!"

Her head reeled. *Is that an Italian accent?*

"And keep still or I'll ram a bag over your head!"

The car took off. Jodie lay still. *They've just turned right.... now left.... now right again.... Geez, how can I work out the direction we're headed in with the car taking so many turns?*

By the time the car pulled up, it was quite dark. "Right, get her out, Aldo."

Jodie's ears prickled. Aldo—Italian? *That accent of the guy speaking, was it Chinese? Or maybe Indian?*

Aldo shoved Jodie in the side with the gun. "You heard—out!"

Large factory-like buildings and warehouses towered above her. *We must be in a light industrial area in outer Perth.*

Aldo grabbed her arm and pulled her in front of him. Then he shoved the gun into the small of her back and frog-marched her into the old red warehouse beside them. The Asian man unlocked a side door, and the three went inside. Forced to climb a flight of stairs, Jodie glanced about in all directions. *I must memorize the layout of this place for later.*

In a small office, Aldo threw her on a chair. "Reckon we need to tie her up, Feng?"

Jodie straightened up. "Who are you? Why are you doing this to me?"

"Talk when you're spoken to, sweetheart. Feng and I have important business to discuss."

"But you've no right to hold me here. I demand to know what's going on."

As Aldo looked at Feng, the Asian man nodded his head slightly. Aldo chucked Jodie under the chin. "A nice-looking girl like you makes a nice bait for a pain-in-the-ass like Marc O'Connors."

The color drained from Jodie's face.

Aldo gave a belly laugh. "How's that for starters?"

"Marc's never done anything to hurt you."

Aldo laughed. "If he kept his nose out of other people's business, he might be a nice guy, but he doesn't."

"Where is Marc?"

"I told you, you're the bait to draw him to us."

"What do you mean?"

"He's disappeared."

Jodie took a deep breath and then exhaled.

"Tell us where he is."

"I don't know."

Roughly Aldo grabbed Jodie's arm and bent it up her back. "You're hurting me!"

"Then tell us what we want to know."

"I don't know—I haven't seen or heard from him for ages."

Feng stepped forward. "Stop pushing her arm."

Heavy footsteps sounded on the stairs. Aldo jumped behind the door and held his gun above his head. Feng drew his gun and pointed it at the door. The door opened and a big man came in. Jodie's eyes widened.

Rex Johns walked up to her. "Jodie, isn't it?"

Feng lowered his gun, and Aldo came out from behind the door.

Adrenalin rushed through Jodie. *Act as if your life depends on him thinking you believe he's your friend, Jodie.* "Oh, Rex, thank goodness you've come! These two men have kidnapped me."

Rex Johns stared at her with an odd look on his face. "Yes, we're sorry about that—I'm afraid we had no choice." He coughed. "These men are police officers."

Jodie's mouth formed a big O. "What?"

Aldo sniggered. Rex Johns shot him a warning look.

Jodie rubbed her elbow. "I thought police were supposed to protect law-abiding citizens from people like that."

An implacable expression on his face, Rex Johns stared at her. "We do if they do what we want."

She raised her eyebrows.

"Unfortunately, recent investigations show Marc's involved in drug trafficking."

Her mouth fell open. "That's not true."

"Yes, we couldn't believe it either. Apparently his amnesia was just a cover for him to extend his drug trafficking."

"That's impossible. He's an honest detective."

Rex Johns shrugged. "Believe it or not, but the facts are there for anyone who wants to see them, and there are witnesses prepared to testify in court against him. I was Marc's partner for some time, and I didn't want to believe it either. But I guess someone made him an offer he couldn't refuse."

Jodie's eyes flashed. *Aren't you talking about yourself?* She bit her lip. "If what you say is true, and I find it hard to believe, what has kidnapping me got to do with it?"

"Marc's on his way here now to do a deal with us to get you back."

Her mouth dropped open again. "How do you know?"

"We put it out through a police grapevine that we were holding you, and even quicker than expected, he got in contact with us."

"What's going to happen now?"

"You play along, and no one will get hurt. Once we've got Marc in custody, you'll be free to go."

"What will happen to him?"

"He'll be arrested for drug trafficking in heroin…" Running footsteps sounded on the stairs. Rex Johns planted his body in front of Jodie's chair. "Ah, that'll be them now."

Them?

The door burst open, and someone raced into the room.

Marc's voice cried, "Okay, Johns, where is she?"

Rex Johns stepped away from Jodie's chair. Beside Marc stood Barney Baker. Jodie paled.

A nerve in Marc's cheek twitched. "Jodie, are you all right?"

She nodded.

Rex Johns held up his hand. "Okay, O'Connors, let's get this over with quickly. You tell me where you've stashed the last heroin shipment, and the girl's yours."

"Where's the guarantee?"

Jodie frowned. *What game are you playing, Marc? I'll try to play along, but I don't want to goof it up for you.*

Rex Johns pointed at Jodie. "Right here. As soon as you produce the information and it's confirmed, you get her."

"I need more than your word for that, Johns."

"Okay, suit yourself. Tie the girl up, fellas."

Barney rushed over to Feng and picked up a rope. Momentarily Jodie closed her eyes. *So you are part of the gang, Barney.*

Marc spun around. "Hey, what's going on, Barney?"

Barney ignored him, and Aldo gestured with his gun for Marc to step back. As Feng bound Jodie's feet, she held them a few centimeters apart. He slapped her hard on the ankle and then drew the sides of the cord together savagely. She yelped and glared at Rex Johns and Barney. "Some police mates you two turned out to be."

Barney walked behind her and tied her hands behind her back. She held them apart and, as he pulled the cord tight, she cried out. *Hey, that didn't hurt at all and I can still move my thumbs.*

Then Barney took a large handkerchief from his pocket and tied it across her mouth. *You could have tied that a lot more tightly too, Barney. Thank you.*

Rex Johns's eyes narrowed. "Right, O'Connor, now are you going to tell us where the heroin is, or do you want us to start shoving your girlfriend around?" He gave Jodie a casual kick on the leg. She squeezed her eyes tight shut. *Beast! That hurt.*

He went to kick her again. Marc stepped toward him. "It's still on the boat. But you'll never find it unless you take me with you."

At a nod from Rex Johns, Barney raised his arm and crashed his gun down on Marc's head. Marc slumped to the floor. Jodie wept. *No, no.* Then Barney bent down and removed a gun from Marc's belt. Jodie threw her bound body at Barney. She missed and landed on the floor. Feng picked her up and threw her up against the wall, and she slid down it.

Rex Johns laughed. "Naughty girl. Been nice knowing you. Pity you picked the wrong sort of guy to get involved with."

He and his three associates left the room. As soon as the door closed, Jodie pushed against the ropes on her feet. *Quick, my feet are losing their feeling already.* The ropes held tight.

She fumbled with the knots binding her hands. *Thank goodness, they're tied loosely near my thumbs.* Her heart leapt. *Perhaps Barney is on Marc's side after all.* But, at the sight of Marc's prostrate body lying in front of her, she shook her head.

Her hands free at last, Jodie ripped off her gag and

started to work on the knots at her feet. Her nose quivered. *What's that?* She sniffed experimentally. *Oh, no, not smoke.* "Marc, wake up, please wake up!"

His good arm moved a fraction. Groaning and holding his bad arm, he groggily pulled himself up into a half sitting position. "Wuz going on? Where am I?" Blinking, he sat blearily looking around the room. "My god, Jodie! Are you all right?"

She continued to fumble with the cord around her ankles. "No, help me. My feet have gone numb, and I can't get this rope off."

He crawled over and pulled at the rope.

Free of her bonds, Jodie rubbed her feet. "Come on, work, damn you."

Marc looked around. "What's that smell?"

"Johns must have set the warehouse on fire. We've got to get out of here fast."

"Take off your jacket and throw it over your head." With his suit coat over his own head, he ran to the door. "Follow me. Don't push the door open more than you have to or the oxygen will fan the fire."

With Jodie hobbling behind, he ran down the already-burning stairs. The bottom two steps were almost burnt through. Marc turned and grabbed Jodie's hand. "We'll have to jump."

"I can't—I'll never make it."

"Jump on *three*! One, two, *three*!" Marc landed on his feet just beyond reach of the flames. Jodie's feet landed in flames. "Marc, my feet won't work!"

Marc pulled her clear and belted the flames licking up her pants with his suit coat.

Jodie gritted her teeth and, with Marc half-dragging her, they raced for the door. Marc grabbed the handle. "It's locked. We'll have to find another way out."

Wildly they looked around. Someone banged on the door. "Marc, is that you?"

Relief flooded Jodie's face. "Tiff!"

Marc bellowed, "Tiff, it's us! We're locked in. Can you smash down the door with something?"

Ryan yelled, "Step back!"

Bang! Bang! Bang! The lock gave, and a hammer came crashing through the door with Ryan attached.

Jodie grabbed Tiff's hand. "Boy, are we glad to see you! I thought the thugs had given you the slip."

"No, we got to your work just as one pushed you out of sight. Ryan followed them here, and we've been watching the comings and goings ever since."

The four raced across the parking lot to Beth's car.

Marc hurled himself into the driver's seat. "Let me drive." His injured arm hanging limply by his side, he switched on the headlights, whirled the car around, and headed back up the street.

Fire brigade sirens screeched as a fire engine tore around the corner toward them. Another screamed after it. A police car followed. Marc slowed his speed.

Once back in traffic, Jodie clenched her teeth and pulled her right foot up and massaged it. "Where are we going, Marc?"

"The docks. Sorry to involve you all in this. Want me to stop and let you out? I can go on alone."

Jodie's nose flared. "You're not dropping me off."

Ryan's eyes hardened. "Nor me."

Tiffany straightened her shoulders. "Nor me."

Grim-faced, Marc accelerated. Before long, the docks came into view. "I'll leave you guys here with the car now and go in on foot." He patted his inside breast pocket. "Good old Barney—he made sure they didn't take my second gun. I might find it useful tonight."

Jodie shuddered.

Chapter 12

Jodie watched Marc merge into the darkness of the dock buildings, and her body trembled. From the back seat, Tiffany leaned over and squeezed her shoulder, and Jodie squeezed her hand back.

Ryan locked the car doors. "Be ready to slide down out of sight if you hear a car approaching."

Tiffany gave a laugh that was half a hiccup. "I don't know whether my nerves can stand this. But it is exciting, isn't it?"

Jodie groaned.

Half an hour later, a gunshot rang out. Jodie's heart skipped several beats, and she peered into the darkness toward the sound.

Suddenly, floodlights and car headlights illuminated the area. Jodie, Tiffany, and Ryan slid down low and froze. More gunshots followed. Men shouted. Police sirens screamed and police cars hurtled past Beth's car onto the docks. An ambulance siren screamed. Jodie wiped her sweaty palms on her slacks.

Some time later, cars drove out from the docks. Jodie was half-lying on the floor in front of the front passenger seat, and Tiff and Ryan sat on the floor in the back.

A car stopped beside their car and someone got out. Jodie held her breath. A man's voice called softly through the window. "It's okay. It's only me."

Her heart gave a lurch, and she shot bolt upright. She unlocked her door and catapulted out of the car into Marc's arms. "Are you all right?"

"Sure." He held her tight and kissed her. Ryan and Tiffany clambered out of the back of the car. Marc grinned. "Good on you, you guys—you were great back-up. We wouldn't have made it without you."

In the semi-dark, a man came up behind Marc and tapped him on the shoulder. Marc turned around and gave the man a grin. "Meet my mate, Barney Baker, the guy to have behind you when the going gets rough."

Jodie sized up the balding blond man in front of her. She licked her lips. "Hello again, Barney."

"Hi, Jodie. Marc tells me I'm not your favorite person."

Without looking directly at him, she took the hand he held out and shook it. "I guess I over-react—any guy who follows me in a car and later smashes a gun over the head of one of my friends has to be a bit suspect with me, I guess."

Marc laughed. "Barney didn't really thump me, Jodie. It was all show."

Barney nodded. "That's right. Marc can fill you in on my role later but, take it from me, he's led a big bust tonight."

Marc smiled a tired smile. "We need to go to the station now to bed some charmers down for the night. Thanks for all your help, Jodie, and you too, Tiff and Ryan. You're real cool guys to have around in a crisis."

Jodie held tight to Marc's hand. "Will you come back to our place later and stay the night?"

Barney laughed. "Sure he will. I'll drop him off there on my way home if you like. Give us a couple of hours."

As soon as they got home, Jodie ran to the phone to ring Eve. "I know it's late, Eve, but I thought you'd want to know Marc is safe."

Out in the back garden Tiffany and Ryan filled in Beth and Tom with what had been happening. Tom shook his head. "If all the bad guys are in custody now, maybe we won't have to worry about bugs in the house any more."

Beth frowned. "It'd probably be worth Marc having a good look around though. We wouldn't want private conversations booming out somewhere we don't know about."

Jodie squeezed her mother's hand.

Later that night, a car pulled into the drive. A few moments later, someone knocked at the door. Jodie rushed up the passage, and then came to an abrupt stop. She peeped through the peephole on the door and then threw the door open. "Marc!" Her body crumpled as he pulled her close and kissed her. "Oh, my darling, I was so scared for you."

As they walked arm in arm into the living room, Beth jumped up. "Hi, Marc. Guess a cup of hot chocolate and some biscuits are just what you need."

Jodie held up her hand and pointed him in the direction of the phone. "Sorry, not yet. You have to ring your mum." She lowered her voice to a whisper. "Then you have to check the room for bugs."

Minutes later Marc rejoined the group, and five expectant faces looked up. He grinned. "What's this—a welcoming committee?"

Tom pointed to a chair. "Come on, none of us is going to get any sleep until you tell us what's been going on."

"Barney was working as a double agent. After he'd won Rex Johns's trust, Johns told him Aldo had followed me into a park by a river where he'd shot at me and reckoned he'd left me for dead."

Jodie shivered. "So it was Aldo."

"Johns also told Barney about you and what he'd learned about you from checking your car rego. Barney followed you to try to find out if I'd really been killed. When I contacted him, we compared notes on what we'd learned about Johns and his drug operations. Because of what I'd learned about the Asian criminals in Port Hedland and knew the ship they'd used for smuggling in their heroin, we were able to access the ship at the docks, steal the heroin, and hide it. Johns thought I was a lone, loose cannon, and why he was so keen to get hold of you and use you as bait to get to me."

Jodie put her hand on Marc's knee, and he covered her hand with his. "When he had you kidnapped, Johns used Barney as the contact to get to me. Johns knew we'd been friends for a long time, so he asked him to spread the message around about the kidnap to a number of people we networked with. Johns named himself as contact person. So it wasn't a surprise to Johns when Barney took me to him."

Jodie gripped Marc's hand. "Why did Barney hit you so hard then?"

"It was a fake smash on the head and I just dropped to the floor."

"He must have hit you or you wouldn't have been knocked out."

"It wasn't the hit that did that. When I slumped to

the floor, I landed on my crook arm and must have blacked out with the pain for a bit."

Jodie pursed her lips. "It looked like a pretty savage hit to me."

"Okay, I admit Barney did have to make it look realistic, or I really would have been a dead duck. But I assure you, he didn't hit my head, and he didn't hurt me."

Ryan leaned forward. "What happened out at the docks?"

Tom tapped his watch "You've got five minutes. Then I'm examining that head."

Marc smiled grimly. "Though we'd stolen the heroin, we hadn't been able to take it off the ship. We'd just stashed it elsewhere on the ship. Barney organized police he trusted to be ready for a bust, whether in Port Hedland, Fremantle, or anywhere else."

"How did he know which police to trust?"

"We knew we had to trust someone, so Barney went to Scott Masters to test him out. When he told him he'd found me and asked him if he should tell Rex Johns where I was hiding, Masters warned him to be careful of Rex Johns and not to let him near me, but to help me hide out until I got my strength back."

Jodie frowned. "Why would he drop Rex Johns in it? I thought they were mates."

"Maybe he was having a bet each way and being a double agent himself until he could be sure which way the wind was blowing."

Tiffany's eyes shone. "Wow. It's just like listening to a movie script, isn't it?"

"Barney told Masters only the minimum of what we thought he needed to know. But he did have to tell him my plan for the big drug bust down at the docks. To make sure we could trust him, Barney told him we'd already confided in several top politicians who would be watching developments with great interest."

Ryan laughed. "Had you really?"

"I'd written a number of letters addressed to myself and posted them here to Jodie and to Mum's." Marc grinned wryly. "On the back of each envelope, I'd written, 'If unclaimed within seven days, please send to...' The first was to the Prime Minister, the second to the Premier, the third to the Federal Minister for Police and the fourth to the State Minister for Police. So, if I hadn't returned in a week, some of my colleagues in the police force would have had some pretty tough questions to answer."

Tiffany clapped her hands.

Tom's mouth twitched. "How did the drug bust itself go?"

"Barney and I had gambled that once Johns learned the heroin was still on the ship, he'd reckon he could find it himself. What he didn't know was we'd organized undercover police to act as crewmen on neighboring boats. They were watching every move. He fell right into our trap."

Ryan grinned. "Great, but what happened after you left us in the car?"

"I headed straight for the smugglers' ship and gave a secret signal to the undercover police. It was dark, and I was able to sneak onto the ship. Most of the crew had gone to bed, so it was virtually only security guys and the guys looking for the heroin I had to worry about."

Jodie clenched and unclenched her fists.

Marc grabbed her left hand and held it tight. "I

surprised Johns poking about in the hold with Aldo and Feng and held them at gunpoint. Barney was with them, but we staged his escape. He went off and found and arrested the two Asian guys I'd busted at Port Hedland."

"What were the shots we heard?"

"When Barney challenged the Asian guys, one of them made a run for it. A police marksman shot at him."

Jodie shivered. "Did he hit him?"

"No, but he stopped him in his tracks."

"Oh, Marc, anything could have happened." She picked up his hand and held it against her cheek. "Any problems when you got to police headquarters?"

"Only for the guys we'd arrested. We opposed bail, so it depends on how good their lawyers are as to whether or not they'll get it."

Jodie gasped. "Surely Rex Johns and his cronies wouldn't get bail."

"Don't worry, they can't touch us. If they're allowed out on bail, there'll be immediate police protection for each of us."

Tom stood up. "That sounds a good place to end the story then." The others stood up, and Tom touched Marc on the elbow. "I think you'd better come into the next room with me and let me have a look at that head of yours now."

After his examination, Tom frowned. "I want you to see the specialist again."

"That's okay—I'm due to see him in a week or so's time anyway."

"No, I mean I want you to see him first thing tomorrow." Marc's face dropped. "I'm not happy you've had two more blows after that first mega one."

Marc shrugged. "But I haven't—not really. Falling out of bed wouldn't have been that bad, and Barney's blow was not even a glancing blow."

"Still not good, I'm afraid. The original swelling there is pretty severe. If you don't object, I'd like to pop into your room several times during the night to see you're just asleep and not unconscious."

Marc put up his hands as if to push Tom away. "Hey, isn't that going a bit far?"

"Not at all. In fact, it wouldn't take much for me to pack you off to hospital this minute and have you kept for observation. So don't tempt me."

****

In the morning Marc told Jodie about her father's misgivings about his head injuries and the appointment he was making for him to see the specialist that morning.

Jodie's face puckered. "And I thought I was the injured one." She showed off rope marks and the myriad small burns on her hands and legs.

"Boy, what have you been up to, growing tiny bubble-gum balloons on your legs?"

Jodie took Marc's face in her hands and gently kissed his lips. "Please look after yourself. I couldn't bear anything more to happen to you."

After breakfast, Tiffany, with Ryan beside her, drove Jodie and Marc to the garage where Jodie's car had been serviced. Ryan jumped out, opened the door for Jodie, and said, "It's going to be boring without you two around when I start back at work on Monday."

Tiffany giggled.

Marc snorted. "If it's thrills you want, contact the

Police Academy and they'll oblige."

Together Ryan and Tiffany threw up their hands. "No way."

****

Jodie drove on to work and then handed her car over to Marc. "As soon as I get in, I'll ring Scott Masters to tell him you'll be late. Don't forget to ring me as soon as you can and tell me what the specialist says."

At her desk she assembled her sketches. Kenny came up and looked over her shoulder. "I think you need a few more paintings."

Two hours later there was a light knock on Jodie's partition. "Marc!" She jumped up and ran to the door. "How did you get on?"

As dejected as a puppy finding his food bowl empty, he sat down. "Not good. I didn't feel like discussing it on the phone, so I decided to come over instead." He looked at the floor. "The specialist has ordered me to quit the police force."

"Ordered you?" Her voice rose to a squeak.

"That's right. He says my days are numbered if I stay. Reckons I've already used up my nine lives, and if I get another bash on the head, I can't expect to get up and walk away again."

Her face tightened. "What are you going to do?"

"Nothing much I can do except accept his advice if I want to stay in the Land of the Living."

"But police work means everything to you."

"Not quite everything." Attempting a smile, he leaned across and clasped both her hands in his.

"Be serious. Let me think—there must be some sort of a compromise."

"I can go onto light duties, but that's not very exciting."

Her eyes brightened. "What's your greatest interest in police work?"

"The criminology aspects, I guess. You know, unraveling the criminal mind. Fascinating stuff."

"Well…"

"Well what?"

"They have teachers in the police force, don't they? So why can't you do a teaching qualification and continue to do what you love through teaching recruits at the Police Academy or teaching members of the force basic and advanced detective skills? If you wanted, you could even go to uni and become a forensic scientist."

Like a kid given his first bike, Marc stared disbelievingly. Then his face split in a huge grin. "Hey, that's not a bad idea. I'll have to check out what qualifications I'd need to do what though."

After seeing him off, Jodie took a deep breath and returned to her desk. She flipped through her sketches and worked on her book.

Packing up at the end of her work day, she gave a big sigh. *Not much to show for a day's work—you didn't have your mind on the job, did you? You should let Marc get on with what he has to do and get on with what you have to do.*

She headed for the bus stop.

At police headquarters, she got off the bus and hurried to where she'd arranged to meet Marc. A man came out of the building. He looked up and gave her a wave. Jodie's heart almost stopped.

He came over. "Hi, Jodie. Looking for Marc?"

She gave a weak smile. "Hi, Barney."

"He told me if I saw you to tell you he was on his way."

She nodded. "Thanks. Any trouble getting out of bed this morning?"

"Tell me about it. Any other job and you'd be given the following day off as a bonus for what we did yesterday. But not the police force."

"I hope you've got this weekend off then."

"Sure thing. Hey, there's Marc coming now." Barney waved to both of them and walked off.

Marc hurried over to Jodie and, her heart pumping like a lovesick schoolgirl's, she tucked her hand inside his arm. "Anything to report?"

"Thanks to the specialist's medical assessment, I've been on light duties since I arrived today. Masters has been making inquiries about me working at the Police Academy, as per your suggestion. Can't fault him really."

Jodie mouth twisted. "Perhaps it's vested interest because he wants you out of his space."

Marc opened the back car door and put his bag and hers on the seat.

Jodie held up her hand. "Hey, have you been over this car for bugs yet?"

"Yep, all clear as of this morning, although I guess anything could have happened this afternoon."

Jodie went to give him a play thump on his bad arm and stopped mid-blow. "Ooh, how's the crook arm today?"

"Pretty good. All that racing driving last night and whatever tested it out. I think I'll survive."

"Want me to drive?"

"It's your car." Jodie climbed behind the wheel and eased the car out into the traffic.

"Want me to tell you the best way to my place?"

She beamed. "You remember?"

"Of course. It's just important things about you I don't."

She blinked away a tear welling in the corner of her eye. "It will be nice to catch up with your mum again. She'll be so pleased to have you back. You give her a hard time, you know."

"It's worse for the guys who are married. Their wives and families get a pretty raw deal of it sometimes."

Jodie glanced across at Marc. He was looking at her intently, and butterflies started up in her stomach.

As they walked up the path at Marc's, Eve opened the door and immediately handed Jodie the phone in her hand. "Phone for you, Jodie. It's your sister."

Jodie took the receiver. "Hi, Tiff. What's up?" She listened intently and frowned. "Sorry, your voice is so high-pitched and excited, I can't understand what you're saying."

"I asked if you had seen the news yet? I saw a preview, so I grabbed a tape and taped the 6 O'Clock News for you, and I've just set up to tape the 7 O'Clock News now."

Jodie raced into the living-room. "Eve, would you mind turning on the television? There's something on you'll want to see."

Marc groaned.

A police reporter stood outside police headquarters in Perth. "Today's major story is last night's big drug bust at Fremantle. With me is a police officer involved in leading the bust."

Eve whirled around to Marc. "That's you. Why didn't you tell us you'd be on the telly?"

Chapter 13

After dinner, Jodie jumped up and grabbed her handbag. "Hey, I just remembered something." She pulled two folders of photos out of her handbag and waved them at Marc. "While we were waiting for you to get back from police headquarters last night, Ryan gave me these."

Eve studied a photo of Joe. Oblivious to the camera, a young tanned man in a tropical setting was shifting a set of sprinklers amongst caravans. "Is that what you looked like as Joe?"

Marc pulled a face. "Never seen the guy before in my life."

Jodie laughed. "That's a photo I didn't know about that the incorrigible Tiff took with my camera."

As Eve worked her way through photos of scenes of Broome, Jodie waved her hand. "Don't worry too much about those."

Eve held one up. "This is a lovely one of you and Marc when he was Joe."

"Yes, Tiff insisted on taking one of us together at Gantheume Point. Joe ordered her to delete it, but obviously she didn't."

Arms crossed over his chest, Marc glowered.

Jodie pointed to another photo. "That one is of Tiff with Ryan and the other boys she got friendly with at Broome."

From the second folder Jodie took out several photos. "Half of these I didn't even know Tiff and Ryan took." She spread out the photos on the table. One showed Joe and Jodie in the water playing ball with the boys. Another showed Jodie painting at her easel and Joe lying beside her on the lawn above Cable Beach.

Eve smiled. "You two are obviously having an earnest discussion about something."

Jodie smiled at Marc. "We must have covered every subject there was to talk about."

His brow furrowed, he studied the photo.

Eve looked up. "Pity Tiff wasn't around with her camera to take a photo of Jodie rescuing you from the river."

"What are you talking about, Mum?"

"You know—when you were shot. Remember, Jodie pulled you out of the river after you nearly drowned?"

"No, I don't remember. I've told you I don't remember anything between getting clouted on the head in Port Hedland to waking up on the floor at the Winters' holiday house after apparently falling out of bed and passing out."

"No need to get agitated. You knew you got a bullet in your arm?"

"Sorry. You're right—you can hardly not know when you've got a hole in your arm."

Eve raised her eyebrows. "Well, you've been told how you got it. Didn't anyone tell you would have drowned if Jodie hadn't dragged you out and resuscitated you?"

Marc turned to Jodie who looked away. "I think it's time I got the full story."

Without embellishment, she told him.

"Why didn't you tell me all that before?"

She shrugged. "Even though I knew you'd lost that part of your memory, it never occurred to me to tell you every single little thing again. Beside, you were so aggressive when you first turned into Marc 2, I wouldn't have had a chance."

Footsteps crunched up the gravel path. Eve pricked up her ears. "Uh, oh, that'll be Linda. Sorry, Marc, but I let slip to her you'd be home tonight. She insisted she would come over after her shift at the hospital."

He groaned. "What a homecoming."

Jodie looked at him speculatively.

"All right, I know what you're thinking, Jodie, and you're right. You're always right, damn it."

As he got up and went to the door, the two women raised their eyebrows at each other.

Through the door came Linda's voice. "Oh, darling, it's so good to see you again."

Jodie jumped up. "How about I wash these dishes?"

Looking uncomfortable, Eve stood up and started clearing the table. As Jodie and Eve were finishing the washing up, the front door shut loudly and Marc stormed out to the kitchen.

Eve looked up. "Was it as bad as that?"

"How do you get through to someone who doesn't want to be got through to?"

Eve put her hand on his good arm. "Has she got the message now?"

"She's got the message there's no engagement. But she's decided that's because I met Jodie and got bewitched by her." Marc threw a look at Jodie and rolled his eyes. "When any attraction for you dies a natural death, as she seems sure it will do, she thinks I'll be there for her—again."

His mother frowned. "That's not good. Would you like me to have a word with her next time I catch up with her?"

"Any offer gratefully received, Mother. Just sort her out and get her off my back—please. Tell her as a kid sister she's just great, but as anything else it's just not on."

****

On Saturday morning after breakfast, Marc took Jodie's hand. "Want to come with me to see all my old haunts?"

At the local primary school, Jodie looked over the fence into its spacious grounds. "So this is where you went to school?"

"Yeah. And if you look closely enough at that banksia over there, you'll see my name at the foot of it. I planted it when I was in Prep."

"Most impressive. I can hardly wait until you show me what you did at high school."

"Right. I'll show you the oval where some kid supposed to be kicking the football kicked me in the hand instead and busted my thumb."

"Is that where you got your love of crime and violence from?"

"No, that was from playing Captain Von Trapp in *The Sound of Music*. But forget the violence stuff—it was more the good guys outwitting the bad guys that appealed to me."

On their return Eve clasped and unclasped her hands. "Are you two doing anything special tonight?"

Marc shrugged. "We haven't got around to sorting anything out yet. Why?"

"If you'd like to go to a dance, there's one on in the Community Hall."

Marc laughed. "There wouldn't be some ulterior motive for your asking, would there?"

Eve colored. "I just thought it might be nice. One of the clients at the clinic mentioned that he goes and says it's always a good night."

"He, eh?" Eve went redder. "I guess that means you'd like to come too."

Jodie gave Marc a soft smack on the forearm. "For goodness sake, Marc, don't be such a tease. I'd love to go, Eve. If Marc's not interested, you and I can go together—how's that?"

"Hey, hey, slow down, I didn't say I wouldn't go. Okay, Mum, what time do we have to be ready?"

****

As Marc paid for the three of them to get in, Jodie looked around. "It must be a popular dance —the hall's near enough to full already. Lots of different of age groups too."

Within minutes, a middle-aged man came up and invited Eve for the first dance. As they moved off into a modern waltz, Marc stood up and put out his hand to Jodie. "May I have this dance?"

She went into his arms. "I wonder if that's the guy your mum knows from the clinic?"

"Well, they certainly seem to be having no trouble making conversation. Anyway, enough about them, it's you I'm interested in." He pulled her tighter. "Know why I decided to come to the dance?"

"Why?"

155

"It was the only way I could think of to get you into my arms."

Jodie punched him lightly on his left arm.

"Hey, that hurt."

"Sorry, sorry. I keep forgetting. Anyway, I guess that puts paid to any ideas you might have been developing."

"Why, is there something I should have in mind?"

"Want another punch on that crook arm?"

At the end of the dance, Eve walked back to Marc and Jodie with her partner and introduced them to each other. The men shook hands. Eve smiled. "Ian comes to these dances every month."

When the music struck up for the next dance, Marc was partway through a story he was telling Ian. A young man stepped in front of Jodie and put out his hand. "Dance?"

Glancing quickly at Marc, Jodie excused herself and walked onto the dance floor with the young man. He whirled Jodie around the floor in a foxtrot, and she followed. As Eve and Ian danced by, Jodie looked around the dance floor. *Where are you, Marc? Oh, no, you're sitting glowering where I left you.*

Jodie's partner smiled down at her. "I'm Antony."

"Hi, Antony. I'm Jodie."

The next time she glanced over to where she had left Marc, he was missing. Some time later, he passed her on the crowded floor. He was dancing with a tall, elegant girl with long black hair. Her full red-and-yellow floral skirt whirled out around her. Jodie's face dropped.

Antony pulled his partner closer, and she pushed her left thumb into his chest.

"How do you like the band, Jodie?"

"Great. Easy to dance to."

After he escorted her to her seat at the end of the dance, Marc came back and sat next to her. He entwined her arm with his good arm and laced his fingers through hers. Jodie groaned. "Sure you wouldn't like me to wear a sign, 'Keep Off. Private Property'?"

Marc lightly kissed her on the lips. "How's this instead?"

"You'll get lipstick on you, and it will serve you right. Anyway, what about that devastating female I saw you with before? You don't want to scare her off too, do you?"

"Who, my old biology teacher?"

"You're joking."

"No, she was my teacher when I was in Year 12, and it was her first year out teaching. She'd have been only about four or five years older than us kids she was teaching. You wouldn't think she had two little kids now, would you?"

A warmth radiated through her.

At the end of the evening, the dancers stood in a circle holding hands and singing "Auld Lang Syne." Then they remained standing for the national anthem.

As people started moving off in all directions, Eve turned to Marc. "Ian's suggested we go for supper now. Would you and Jodie like to come with us?"

"No thanks, Mum, I think we'll run ahead—we've still got some sleeping to catch up on." Marc glanced at Jodie. "Haven't we?"

She nodded.

"I presume Ian will be happy to drive you home."

Ian came up behind him. "Sure thing."

Eve smiled up into his eyes, and he tucked her hand inside his arm.

Jodie settled back in Marc's car and pulled on her seatbelt. "Ian seems a nice guy."

"I hope so—Mum deserves only the best."

"Hey, he's only asked her out to supper."

"I didn't even ask you out to supper, and look where I've ended up."

Tingles ran down Jodie's body into her toes, and her toes curled. "And where exactly is that?"

Marc grinned and lightly pinched her knee.

In the semi-darkness of Eve's living-room, Marc's lips searched Jodie's face as she cuddled next to him on the couch. His lips traversed her ears, eyelids, and neck. Jodie groaned. "What are you trying to do—get me to fly?"

As Marc pushed her down until her back was flat on the couch, Jodie groaned again. He kissed her hairline. "I love you, Jodie. I love you."

"Oh, Joe, I love you too."

"Joe?" Abruptly Marc pulled himself back and sat up. "Just who is it you love, Jodie—me or someone who doesn't exist anymore?"

While he sat staring at her in the darkened room, she mouthed words, but no sound came. She put her hand up to his face and took deep breaths. "Joe's not dead, Marc—he's part of you. He's the reason I'm here with you now."

"But I'm not that stranger you met in Broome. I'm me—I'm Marc."

"You're making this very hard for me. I can't deny the love I felt for you when you were Joe, or when you were Marc, and now when you're Marc 2. I know you aren't quite the same person as Joe or Marc—not in looks or personality, but they're both part of you."

His sullen face stared back at her.

"For goodness sake, how can you be jealous of yourself?"

Slumping forward on the couch, he dangled his hands between his knees. "Oh, god, I wish I could remember everything about us, everything we did and said before."

"I do too. Didn't lying here before bring back any memories of us together in Broome?"

Leaning across, he kissed her behind each ear. "Sometimes I get little flickers as though some memory has been triggered off and I am coming close to remembering." He kissed her eyelids. "Please tell me everything—knowing might help bring it all back."

Wreathed in semi-darkness, Jodie told him how they met, of their days on Cable Beach, of their days when she painted or sketched and he lay beside her reading and of the night of the cyclone.

"I do wish I could remember." He pressed his face into her hair. "I'd love to have shared those times with you."

"You did." She groaned and pushed him away. "Then we drove down the coast together. You must remember showing me where the Aboriginal guys picked you up and then the track where you had been dumped and left for dead. We walked along the bush track to where you'd been buried under branches and leaves."

Brooding, he shook his head.

"What about that night we stayed in a cabin at Port

Hedland?" Her stomach contracted. *Oh, Marc, it is so hard to tell you what we did when you have so little memory of it, if any.*

Marc kissed her cheeks. "My poor darling, I've made you cry. I'm so sorry I'm making this so tough for you. It is a beautiful love story, and I'm so glad you shared it with Joe and not someone else."

Her face buried in Marc's chest, she sobbed. "I am too, and it is just so frustrating to be bursting with love for a man who can't remember the moments we've shared."

After a time he lifted her hand, kissed the inside of her palm and then the inside of her wrist. She trembled. "Stop it, or you'll make me fly."

He kissed the inside of her wrist again. "Now tell me about my change into the two Marcs."

Jodie blew her nose and sat up straight. "It was funny. As Joe, you were a quiet, casual sort of guy getting round in an old pair of jeans and not much else. Tiffany thought you were a handsome young spunk with your long, dark, curly hair and five o'clock shadow."

"What did you think?"

"Oh, I came around to her way of thinking in time." She gave him a wicked grin. "Like in about ten seconds. Then, when you, uh, Joe, decided to come to Perth with me, he let his beard grow."

Rubbing his still-bearded face up her cheek, Marc laughed. "My one concession to the lost days."

"Even though you had no memory of your earlier life, once you knew your name was Marc instead of Joe and you knew who you were and what your job was, you changed. When you went back home and met your mum, you changed even more. I was confused, but I still loved you, and you still seemed to want me around. But it was as if I had to get used to your being another person. For a start, you started wearing different clothes—smart casual clothes."

"That was what I had in my wardrobe at Mum's."

"There was more to it than that. You seemed to have more purpose in life."

"You lost your hippie?"

"I guess so."

"Did you love Marc?"

"I still loved Joe, and Marc was all I had of him. It was as if Marc was showing me another side of Joe's personality."

"But did you love Marc for himself?"

"When he was shot at the river, I nearly went crazy—it made me realize I loved him whether he was Joe or Marc or some strange mix, and I couldn't bear to lose him."

"What about Marc 2?"

"Oh, him?" Jodie flicked her hand dismissively and looked up at Marc, her eyes wide and luminous in the darkened room. "He's so bad-tempered, you wouldn't believe. I don't know why he turns me on, but he does." She reached up and pulled his face down to hers. "Is that enough interrogation for one night?"

"Guess it will have to be. I can hear a car pulling into the drive, and we'll be disturbed by the young lovers if we don't get a move on."

Jodie hurried off down the passage.

****

As Jodie and Marc were finishing breakfast, Eve came out. A deadpan expression on his face, Marc

161

turned to her. "Hi, sleep well?"

"Yes, thanks."

"How'd you and Ian make out last night?"

Eve went pink. "Good."

"Good? Is that all we're going to get?"

"What do you want me to say?"

"Well, here were Jodie and I waiting up for you. What were we to think when you didn't land home until one in the morning?"

With a warning glare at Marc, Jodie turned to Eve. "Don't take any notice of him—he's just jealous."

Eve smiled. "Ian's lovely. But his family has had a tough time of it with cancer like we have. Two years ago, his wife died of breast cancer. Since then, he's been a bit of a lost soul. Although he shifted to a unit over here to be nearer his sons, it hasn't really worked out. His sons have got their own lives to live, and although Ian keeps himself busy, he gets very lonely at times."

Jodie shook her head. "It must be rough."

Marc put on a fake innocent expression. "Are you seeing him again?"

His mother's face grew pinker. "That's what I wanted to talk to you about. Would you mind if I invite Ian to come on our drive today? He'd love to walk around King's Park with us. He's a native plant man, and they've got lots of native plants there."

Marc winked at Jodie. "I bet you've already invited him."

"I saw that. For your information, I told him we'd pick him up at ten."

Jodie grinned. "Good for you, Eve."

Marc glanced at his watch. "Better get moving

then."

****

At the lookout overlooking the city of Perth and the Swan River, Eve took a photo of Jodie and Marc against a backdrop of the city's skyscrapers.

Marc put out his hand for the camera. "Thanks, Mum. Your turn now."

As they posed, Ian put his arm around a smiling Eve's shoulders.

As they followed Ian and Eve around the hilly gardens, Marc squeezed Jodie's hand. "I've been thinking about everything you said last night."

She nodded.

"On the way back to your place tonight, could we detour via the park by the river? I'd like you to show me where everything happened there."

Jodie's throat tightened. "I can't. It was terrible going through it—I don't want to have to relive it."

"I'm sorry, but I don't know how I can retrieve my lost memories if I don't have as many prompts as I can get."

Jodie gritted her teeth and looked down. "Okay, if we have to, we have to."

"I just wish we could flip up to Broome and have a look around there too."

****

Jodie and Marc stood on the river bank looking down to a large tree trunk that had fallen into the river downstream. "Mean anything to you?"

Marc shook his head.

"After Aldo shot you here, that's the tree trunk that stopped you drifting farther downstream."

"I've no direct memory of it, but I do have a sense

of foreboding—that this is a bad place, that something bad happened here."

"Your gut feeling at work again?"

Marc spent the night at Jodie's, and the following morning Jodie dropped him off at a bus stop.

That evening he beat Jodie home. "Hope you don't think you've got a permanent boarder, Beth."

Beth offered him a cup of tea. "It's nice to have you here. Besides, I've never seen Jodie happier."

"Mum says the same about me. Can't think why."

They both grinned.

****

At the end of the evening meal, Jodie stood up. "Like to go for a walk, Marc?" *Say yes or I'll burst.*

His eyes bright as though repressing his own excitement about something, Marc nodded.

As soon as the front door shut behind them, Jodie blurted out, "Guess what. Kenny wants me to fly to Broome this weekend."

Marc mouth fell open. "What? Why?"

"Today he went through my Broome book. He's always reckoned something was missing from it. Now he reckons he's worked out what it is—it's paintings of the Shinju Matsuri Festival."

"The what?"

"You know, the Shinju Matsuri Festival—the Festival of the Pearl. It's an annual festival that celebrates the pearling industry and Broome's multi-cultural heritage. They put on a big street parade with the Chinese dragon and all that."

"When is it?"

"This year it's in August. Kenny got me to ring up the Broome Information Center today, and guess what?"

Marc shook his head.

"It starts this weekend and goes for ten days. How's that for timing? Kenny wants me to go up to paint it. Isn't that fabulous?"

Marc's face dropped. "But weren't you coming to stay at my place?"

"Silly, I still want to be with you. I want you to come to Broome with me. Didn't you say something about wishing you could go back to Broome to retrace your steps?"

"Yes, but…"

"Well, here's your chance."

"Gee, I don't know if I could…"

"If money's the problem, forget it. Kenny's paying all my expenses—so that's my travel and the bulk of our accommodation sorted out. All we have to do is find the money for your plane ticket and any gap between single and twin accommodation. Given you're on light duties, you should be able to get time off from work. What do you reckon?"

Marc grinned. "What's with this twin accommodation? What's wrong with double?"

"Quit being a smart guy, and tell me what you think."

"Sounds wonderful. But, gee, all that makes my news a bit of an anti-climax."

"What news? Tell me."

"The department's decided to look favorably on my request to train police recruits and detectives and they want me to get teaching qualifications and to study criminology at uni as well."

"Wonderful!" Jodie threw her arms round him.

"When do you start?"

"Uni won't start until next year, but they reckon they can find work for me at the academy almost immediately."

Jodie looked as though she had swallowed a fly. "Does that mean you won't be able to come with me to Broome?"

"Don't look so down. If my brain specialist reckons the trip could help my amnesia, then maybe I could get ten days off on sick leave."

"But Scott Masters thinks you've got your memory back already."

"Don't fret—we'll work something out."

They rushed back and told Tom, Beth, and Tiffany their plans. Tom cleared his throat. "Er, umm, if you need a bit of a loan to get you up there, Marc, just say."

"It's okay, thanks. All my police pay for the two months I was up in Broome is sitting in my bank waiting for me, along with my earlier savings. There's even talk of compensation because I was injured in the line of duty."

In an exaggerated fashion, Tiffany glowered at them. "Half your luck. How about Ryan and I stow away in your luggage?"

Chapter 14

As the plane touched down in Broome, Jodie clutched Marc's arm. "I don't know whether to be excited or scared out of my mind." He kissed her lightly on the nose, and she affected a long-suffering look. "You might be acting Mr. Cool, but I can sense you've got a coiled spring inside you just like I have. You're taking in every detail as we're landing, aren't you?"

Driving through Broome in their hire car, Jodie pointed out various buildings and parks to Marc.

He frowned. "Nup, nothing."

"How about the warm sun and the swaying palms? Are they stirring any memories?"

Stony-faced, he shook his head again.

When they approached Gilbert's Caravan Village, Jodie gave a giggle.

Marc raised an eyebrow. "What's so funny?"

"I'm dying to see if Gilbert recognizes you."

"Give me a break."

Inside the entrance to the caravan park after they had booked in, Gilbert rode up on his motorbike. He stared at Jodie and the on-site van key she held out to him.

"Don't I know you?"

"Possibly, I stayed here once."

Ignoring Marc with his neat beard and short hair, Gilbert smiled his sycophant smile. "Always pleased to welcome back satisfied customers. You were very lucky to get an on-site van at less than a week's notice, you know—Broome's crowded out for the festival."

"Really? It looks pretty crowded here anyway."

With a snort, Gilbert turned the wheel of his motorbike and led the way toward their van.

Marc laughed. "As you reckon they've given you the old van you had before, I guess we can presume it's the worst van in the place."

"You're getting sarcastic about your old mate Gilbert already. That's a good sign."

He pulled a face.

Jodie pointed. "There's your old tent, just as it was before the cyclone. Ring any bells?"

"Nup, but I believe everything you told me about it."

Gilbert rode off, and Marc hurried into the van and looked around.

Jodie came up behind him. "Anything?"

"Nup, still nothing."

A man in his seventies emerged from the tent next door. Jodie laughed. "Looks like Gilbert must have decided the young were unreliable." The man went over and moved the set of sprinklers. "Take fifty years off that guy and turn back the clock a month or so, and that's you."

"Oh, my god!" Marc covered his eyes. Something hit him in the face. "Hey, what was that?"

"Your old jeans to put on. I got them from your mum and packed them to help make everything about this trip as authentic as possible. Perhaps you'd better shave off your beard now and then leave off shaving to allow a five o'clock shadow to develop."

He threw the jeans back at her.

****

Sitting on the sand in his old jeans at Town Beach eating salad rolls with Jodie, Marc studied the festival program. "Competitions, displays, a beach carnival, and a food fair." He paused to take another bite of roll. "Hey, this sounds really good—dragon-boat races and a grand finale with fireworks and dancing."

"Right, and does it say anything about a parade? That's what I've really come for."

"Yep. If you like, you can also go to the Chinese Feast of Hung Ting to honor the dead, the crowning of the Shinju Queen ball, and two Mardi Gras."

"At that rate we could go flat out for the whole ten days. But when would I get any painting done?"

"And when would you go over the old haunts with me?"

The two spent the next few hours wandering round Chinatown and Streeter's Jetty and then the Japanese and Chinese cemeteries and Pioneer Cemetery. Marc threw up his hands. "Truce, I give up."

"What do you mean?"

"I've got history coming out of my eyes and ears. How about we just flake on the beach for the rest of the day?"

"Not a bad idea. We've got to get our energy back to go to the Mardi Gras tonight anyway."

Marc groaned.

****

That night they made their way through a brightly-dressed throng of people. Marc squeezed Jodie's hand. "We'll keep it low-key, eh? I just want to sus the place out and see who's around and what's going on."

A big Indigenous man in his late forties passed Marc and immediately turned back and placed his hand on his shoulder. "Joe!" He gave Marc a big smile. "It's me, Lucas—you can't have forgotten me?"

"Of course not, Lucas." Marc pulled Jodie beside him. "This is my girlfriend, Jodie."

She held out her hand and shook Lucas's hand. Lucas turned around. "Hey, fellas, it's Joe.'' Four more Indigenous men joined them.

Lucas lowered his voice. "Everything okay now? You ever find the skunk who hit you?"

Marc shook his head.

"There are some bad guys around. Us older blokes shoot 'em off quick smart when we see 'em, but they always trying to get at our young fellas and girls."

"What do they want?"

Lucas glanced about. "Don' you remember? I tol' you before." He lowered his voice to a whisper. "To 'ook 'em on dope."

"What sort?"

"Any sort o' dope you can name."

"Heroin?"

Lucas nodded.

"Do you know the names of any of the drug-pushers?"

"No, but I know what they look like."

Marc nodded. "Where do they try to get at the young people?"

"In the streets, pubs, anywhere."

"Do they ever come to your camp?"

Lucas gave a distorted laugh. "Did once, 'til we told 'em we'd sic the dogs on 'em if they ever came again."

Lucas promised to catch up again before Marc returned to Perth, and then he and his friends moved on. Jodie looked at Marc's face. "Ring any bells?"

Ruefully he punched his forehead lightly. "No, damn it."

"You're a good actor then."

"Thanks. Didn't see any point in going into a long story at this stage."

"Lucas and his friends seem to be nice guys."

"Must have been. They saved my life—so you tell me." The furrows in Marc's forehead deepened.

That night Jodie arrived back from the showers before Marc and climbed into her old bed. A few moments later she heard him come in and lock the door. His bunk bed creaked as he crawled into it. "Is this how it was the night of the cyclone?"

"Yes."

"Then what?"

"Some time later, you woke me up with your yelling."

"Like this?" Marc gave a soft experimental yell.

"Be quiet. You'll have us thrown out of the park."

"No, that's not what you said happened. You're supposed to jump up and come over to my bed and fall on top of me."

"There's not much wrong with your memory."

"Just learned it off by rote from you. Well, are you coming over or not?"

"In your dreams." As if cooling down from the heat. Jodie waved her hand back and forth in front of her face. *Boy I'll shoot the top of my head off if I keep pushing down the suppressed excitement I'm feeling.*

"Okay, we'll take that as read. Now it's my turn to

come over to your bed, right?"

In the gloom of the van, Marc jumped out of his bunk and made his way over to the double bed. He pulled back the bedcovers and went to hop in. Jodie put up her hand in a stop sign. "Hold on, chum. No one said this was part of the deal."

"I thought the whole idea of this trip was for us to recreate past events to try to stimulate my memory. Personally, I can't think of anything more likely to stimulate my memory than reliving the night of the cyclone, can you?" Wickedly, he grinned and pressed his mouth on hers before she could answer.

Jodie felt her defenses weaken. *How I'd love to let my whole body mold itself against yours.*

He lay on her and pulled her body full length against his own.

"You make it very hard."

Her face being smothered with kisses, she lay wrapped in his arms. Myriad sensations flooded through her. *All my rational impulses are telling me to call it off before it's too late, but it is so hard.*

His caresses became more demanding. "Oh, Jodie, I love you."

"I love you too." Weakly she tried to push him away, but he continued his caresses. "No, Joe, no!"

Abruptly he dropped his hands from her body and rolled onto his back. "I've told you before, I'm not Joe."

Not speaking, Jodie rolled onto her back, not touching him. Her eyes prickled and she blinked hard. After several minutes of silence, she turned onto her side away from him and closed her eyes.

It was light when she awoke and felt around next to

her. "Where are you, Marc?" She looked around. Quickly she jumped out of bed and pulled on her clothes.

On the way to the amenities block, she passed him coming back. She gave him a tremulous smile. "Hi."

****

Driving along the road to Cable Beach, Marc checked his inside and outside rear-vision mirrors. Jodie leaned forward and looked in her outside passenger mirror.

Marc glanced across at her. "What are you doing, Jodie?"

"The same as you." She glared. "All right, I'm getting as paranoid as you are."

At the sight of Cable Beach's long, white sands, her throat contracted. She took a quick look at Marc's face. "Have you ever seen such a beautiful beach?"

Marc shook his head. "No, and I can't wait to try it out."

Oh, Marc, surely you can remember something about the place where we spent so many hours getting to know each other.

They splashed around in the water and swam for half an hour and then lay down on their backs on their beach towels. A smile on her face, Jodie exhaled. *Gee, you look so tempting there, Marc, I'd love to rub my hand down your tanned torso. Don't you feel like reaching out to me too?*

He continued to lie passively, his face and his eyes shielded by his sunhat and sunglasses.

Are you still moping about the Joe/Marc thing? If you are, it's time you genuinely appreciated that Joe is part of you. If you can't accept it, that's just too bad because I'm not going to try to deny the love I had for him and still have.

After a rest, Jodie suggested they try the Vine Thicket Walk.

Marc pulled on his jeans over his togs. "Sounds like a jeans job."

At the car, they dropped off their towels and other gear. Then they headed off to the start of the walk. Marc bent in a crouching position and took off. "Race you to the start!"

Jodie's mouth dropped open. She tore after him. A hundred meters along the track, he stood with his hands on his hips waiting. She caught up to him. "Well?"

"Well, what?"

"Your memory must be coming back."

"Why do you say that?"

"You remembered where the start of the track was."

"Sorry, but I saw it from the car when we drove past before."

Her face puckered, and she pulled away and ran off along the track. Slowly Marc followed and stood next to her as she knelt studying a plant.

She didn't look up. "You can eat this one, you know. The Aborigines reckoned it was good bush tucker."

"Jodie, we need to talk." Gently he stood her up and turned her to face him.

"No, we don't. Everything that went before obviously means nothing to you. You don't want Joe to have existed. Okay, if he didn't exist, then neither did much of our relationship so we start from scratch now, okay? I don't know you, and you don't know me."

"No, don't be like that. I love you." He went to kiss her, but she pulled away and ran farther along the track. Hands in his pockets, Marc scuffed a few bits of stone and trailed along after her.

Her face ashen, she slowed down and glanced back at him. *The day's lost its gloss as far as I'm concerned, and you don't look much happier than I feel. Well at least you look like Joe now—like a confused lost boy.*

On the way back to the caravan, they stopped to pick up fish and chips. As they shared them in the van, Jodie stretched out her legs. "Nothing like fish and chips on holiday, is there?"

"Guess not."

She closed her eyes and raised her eyebrows. *This is going to be a great night.*

As they tidied up after tea, Jodie glanced at Marc's somber face. "Want to go for a walk?"

They walked to the boom gates. Marc looked up and down the road. "Which way do you want to go?"

"If we go to the right, we'll follow the road past the far end of the caravan park and on to where those hoons tried to get me into their car that time."

He threw her a questioning look.

"No, of course you don't remember—it didn't happen, did it?"

Marc grabbed her by the elbows and turned her to face him. "I'm sick of you picking at me because I can't remember things. I can't help it if I don't remember."

"I'm not picking at you. I'm just fed up with you acting as though I've no right to have loved Joe and to still love him. If you can't remember, that's your bad luck, but don't try to deny me my memories."

"That's not my intention at all. I'm sorry if that's

what you think. I just get so frustrated that I can't remember."

"Well, it's ridiculous for you to be jealous of yourself."

"I'm not jealous of myself—just jealous, if that's the right word, of not being able to remember the good times we shared. Forgive me?"

Jodie looked into his eyes. "Maybe." Pulling him by the hand, she strode along the side of the road. "Come on, let's see if we can drum up some memories."

Although she pointed out the various places she remembered things happening the last time they did the walk, he looked blank. She threw up her hands. "Okay, let's call it all off."

"Call what off?"

"We're both trying too hard. The pressure on you to recall everything is just too much. From now on, I'm not going to ask, 'Do you remember?' If you've ever got anything to tell me, just tell me, right?"

"Right."

That night Jodie thrashed around in her bed. *Thanks for not complicating things by trying to join me, Marc. Much as my body aches to lie with yours, all my survival instincts are telling me this isn't the time.*

Chapter 15

The parade route was crowded with locals and tourists. As they walked along, Jodie looked about her. "Kenny must be mad if he expects me to sit and paint the parade."

Marc stopped. "How about this for a good spot to watch it?" They set up their camp stools and sat down.

Jodie flipped open her sketch pad. "Hope you won't be too self-conscious sitting next to me sketching away."

"No, but I hope no one's looking at me and recognizing me."

"Lucas did. Who else would know you're here?"

"Don't look now, but two Chinese-looking guys across the street turned up shortly after we sat down, and they haven't taken their eyes off me."

Casually, Jodie glanced across. She licked her lips and turned a page of her sketch book. With deft strokes, she quickly sketched the likenesses of the two slightly-built men in charcoal. Looking down, Marc let out a whistle. "With you around, who needs a camera?"

Band music sounded in the distance and then came closer and closer. A huge Chinese dragon, its bright rainbow-striped body with scores of people forming its legs, gyrated toward them. Jodie's eyes shone. "Isn't it great?"

"When you point your camera again, can you make

sure you pick up those two guys in some of your shots? Unobtrusively, of course."

****

After the parade, Marc picked up their stools and started to move off into the crowd. Jodie picked up her painting gear. "Don't you want to wait until the crowd thins?"

"No, those two characters are still taking too great an interest in us. Come on, let's move."

They weaved in and out of groups on the footpath and road, and Jodie glanced behind. Her throat constricted. "You're right, the two men are following us."

Marc glowered. "Damn having to park the car so far away."

"Why not take it easy? What can they do? They can't attack us in broad daylight, and once we get into the open, they'll be on show. If they don't want us to see them, they'll be the ones having to take the evasive action, not us."

"Good thinking." Marc steered Jodie into a store. For ten minutes or so they browsed around inside and bought several souvenirs.

Then they went outside again. The two men who had been stalking them were leaning against the side of the store next door.

Marc jutted out his jaw. "Okay, they've asked for it." Quickly he led the way to their rental car. They threw in their gear, climbed in, and drove off. The two men stood and watched them drive off.

Marc laughed. "Not sure what's going on there. We must have caught them napping. I'd have thought they'd have a car ready and waiting within cooee of ours."

"Where are we going?"

"I'm parking opposite the post office but we're really going to the police station up the street a bit." Jodie shot him a questioning look. "It's time we got a few things sorted out. Make sure you bring your sketch pad with you."

At the police station, Marc introduced himself and Jodie, and they were ushered into Sergeant Nakamura's office. An officer of a mixed Asian background in his mid to late thirties sat behind the desk. He spoke with a strong Australian accent. "Yes, drugs aren't a big problem here as far as we know, Detective Constable, but we have heard whispers."

"Any idea who's involved?"

"We suspect there's an Asian connection. However, in a multi-cultural town like Broome, there are so many people with so many different connections with so many different Asian countries, it's difficult to pin down exactly which persons are involved."

"You have your suspicions, though?"

"Yes, but no proof."

"You haven't got any witnesses?"

"They exist, but none who are willing to stand up in court and point the finger."

"Understandable." Marc reached across for Jodie's sketch pad. "Do you know these two men?"

The sergeant studied the sketch. "I certainly do— they're the Wong brothers." He turned to Jodie. "You drew them?"

She nodded.

"They're very good likenesses. Where did you see them?"

"They spent the whole morning eyeing us off from the other side of the street at the parade."

"Why?"

Marc frowned. "That's what we want to know. I'm here on holiday, not on police business, and Jodie's not in the police force at all."

"Perhaps someone gave them a tip-off you'd be here."

"That's a worry, but it's the most likely explanation." He looked thoughtful. "Can you find out if either of the Wongs has a police record, Sergeant?"

Marc and Jodie headed back to the car. She tapped him on the arm. "What now?"

"I've got a few things I want to check out. What did you want to do?"

"I want to drop this film off for developing. I saw a place that advertises they do films in an hour. While I was waiting, I thought it would a good chance to do some shopping."

"Okay, how about I drop you off and go off for the hour to do what I have to do?"

Jodie bit her lip. "Remember what your brain specialist said—you can't afford to take any more risks."

An hour later, Jodie stood outside the shopping center with a trolley of groceries and a folder of snaps. While she waited, she flipped through the folder. *Ah, the Chinese dragon.* She smiled to herself. *That's the one.* She stared at a photo of the head of the dragon turning front on to the camera with the full length of its colorful body in view alongside. *That's the one I'm going to paint.*

A car drove past her, and, as the driver waved and

turned into a nearby parking spot, she glimpsed his grim expression. *Uh, oh, what now, Marc?*

Jodie hurried over with her trolley. Marc lifted up the lid of the car boot and helped her pile in her shopping. "What's up?"

"Tell you in the car."

As he drove along, a small nerve twitched in his cheek. "After I dropped you off, I went looking for Lucas and found him and some of his friends in a park. I showed him your sketch of the two guys eyeing us off at the street parade, and he identified one as the guy who'd tried to flog drugs to him."

"Oh, dear."

"Mind waiting in the car while I slip up to the police station again? I want to check if Sergeant Nakamura's got anything on the Wongs yet."

"Want to show him these too?" Jodie produced the folder of photos from her handbag.

Marc shuffled through the photos of the street parade. "Not bad at all."

While he was gone, Jodie studied the people going past. *Boy, what a great variety of peoples live here. No wonder it's such a cosmopolitan town.*

When Marc returned, he handed the photos back to Jodie. "No doubt about it—the two guys we saw were the Wong brothers. Your pics of them confirmed it. Though the sergeant has a list of offenses they've been charged with, none of them has ever stuck." He frowned.

"What?"

"Nothing much, but he also warned me to be careful in any dealings with them. Their father's a very powerful man in Broome."

"In what way?"

"In any way you care to name. Apart from pearling, he's into real estate and owns a number of the big businesses in town that he or his relatives manage or rent out to a select few. One of his relatives is in federal politics and is rumoured to have numerous overseas connections in both Asia and Europe, as does Mr. Wong himself."

"Hmm, the local Mr. Big by the sound of it. Would Sergeant Nakamura have a photo of him to show you, do you think?"

"He already has. Here." Marc handed across a photocopy of a photo from a local paper.

Jodie stared at a slightly-out-of-focus photo of a stocky Chinese man in his early sixties. She shrugged. "Nothing out of the ordinary."

Marc pulled out of the car park.

"What are you going to do now?"

"For a start we'd better get back to the van and unload our groceries before they melt in this heat. And I guess you want to start painting sometime."

"Correct."

"While you paint, I'm going to make more inquiries. I want to catch up with Lucas again, and I think it might be time to give Barney a ring."

Jodie's stomach plummeted.

With Marc gone, Jodie set up her easel and worked from her photos and sketches. *Great that Marc's so fired up and wants to find answers to questions, but I do hope he's okay.* She shivered. *I can't bear to even think about what the Wongs might be plotting.*

Soon engrossed in her task, she layered streaks of bright yellow onto her Chinese dragon. *This will be one of the most striking paintings in the book.*

Some time later, Jodie glanced at her watch. *Nearly five thirty. Time to pack up. Where are you, Marc?* As she placed the photos of the dragon back in their folder, she caught sight of a photo with the Wong brothers in the background and gave an involuntary shudder.

As she chopped up vegetables for tea, a car approached and pulled up outside the van. Quickly, she dried her hands and hurried and opened the door. *No car I recognize.* She put her hand up to her heart. *Stop thumping so hard.*

A man climbed out of the car and came toward her. "Marc!" She rushed over and pulled him into the van. There she reached up and put her hands around his neck. "I'm so glad you're back."

"If I get a homecoming like this every time I go away, I'll go away again." He pulled her close and kissed her as though he were her long-lost lover.

Finally, she pulled away. "Phew. Perhaps you'd better tell me what's with the new car."

"You noticed. I'll make a detective of you yet." She threw a punch at him, and he dodged it. "I wasn't happy the Wongs would have the description and registration number of our rental car, so I stopped off at the hire car place and made an excuse to change cars. I told them we needed a bigger one."

"Good thinking. What else happened?"

"I got onto Barney, and he's going to see about pulling a few strings and getting up here as soon as he can."

Jodie's mouth tightened.

"You still don't trust him, do you?"

"It's not that—I hardly know him. I guess he gave

me such a fright the night he followed me and again when I saw you in the car with him, it sort of started our relationship off on the wrong foot. Seeing him brain you with a gun at the warehouse didn't help either."

"I told you he didn't brain me. It was all pretend." He held her shoulders and looked into her eyes. "If he was crooked, we wouldn't be here now."

Jodie pulled away. "We nearly weren't. He left us locked in a burning warehouse, remember?"

"He didn't know about that—he and Johns had gone ahead to the car. Aldo and Feng organized the rest."

"On Rex Johns's orders?"

"Who else's? Anyway, even if Barney had known about it, he couldn't have done anything without blowing his own cover."

Jodie shrugged.

"Besides, he would have known we'd have got ourselves out because he hadn't hit me at all and he'd tied you up so you could get free."

Jodie snorted. "He might have tied me up a bit more loosely then, and I don't know about not hitting you."

"He had to make it look convincing."

"Thanks to Barney for small mercies, I guess. But that still wouldn't have got us out of the locked building before we'd have been burned to death. If it hadn't been for Tiff and Ryan..." She gave a shudder. "Anyway, given all the other things that have happened, you must be right about Barney. I do want to believe in him as much as you do—you desperately need a friend in the police force you can trust."

"Yeah, you can't watch your own back—that's

why I'm so savage about Johns and so wary of Masters."

Jodie nodded. "How did you get on with Lucas?"

"Good. He took me around his camp and introduced me to a lot of the people there, especially the young guys. I was very impressed with his son, Ben. He wants to be a police officer, and I told him I'd do what I could for him."

"You're a lovely man, you know that?"

He cupped his ear. "What was that? Can you speak a bit louder, please?"

****

The next day Marc went off, and Jodie worked on her paintings some more.

On his return she ran out to the car. "Well?"

"Nothing much to report. Sergeant Nakamura and I are working closely together, and the Aboriginal community is being very cooperative."

After dinner Marc and Jodie walked up to the phone box outside the caravan park kiosk. Jodie stood outside while Marc rang. "Hi, Barney, it's me. How'd you get on organizing that holiday in Broome?"

A few minutes later Marc emerged with a big smile on his face. "Back-up's on its way. He reckons he was able to swing it and will be here tomorrow morning."

"Aren't you worried someone might have been listening in to your call, or that Scott Masters might have tipped off someone up here?"

"Of course, but I didn't have much choice except I took the precaution of sending off another set of letters to politicians care of Mum and your parents in case anything goes wrong."

"What if Scott Masters knows enough to have

someone in Broome intercept any mail sent to them?"

"I thought of that, so I sent one to Ryan as well."

"Good old Ryan."

"What do you want to do now?"

"Go to bed and get a good night's sleep."

Snuggled up alone in her double bed Jodie smiled. *Good you're keeping to your own bed, Marc. Tonight my dreams are going to be of Joe and the dolphins and our time together in Broome.*

Chapter 16

A young woman with short black hair and Grecian features walked up beside Barney from the plane to the exit gate. Marc waved to them and rushed to hug the woman. "What a surprise you are!"

Jodie blinked several times. *Wow, who's the gorgeous lady and what is she to Marc?*

Marc led the woman to her. "This is Jodie, my girlfriend. Jodie, this is Helena, Barney's wife."

A broad smile swept across Jodie's face. *Thank goodness for that. Now Linda's been sorted out, I couldn't cope with some other female complication.*

Helena held out her hand. "Hope it doesn't put you out to have me here but, since my mum was free to mind the kids at short notice, here I am."

Marc laughed. "Helena's a detective too. Although she took time off when her children were very young, she came back part-time a few months ago."

Jodie smiled warmly at her. *Not happy about another woman sharing Marc's dangerous life though.*

With a grin, Barney came up behind his wife. "Lost any tails lately, Jodie?"

"No, I leave that to the cat with nine lives—when he's not nursing a bullet in his arm or a busted head. Anyway, what are you doing in that jumper? You'll die of heat exhaustion within minutes."

"It was only sixteen degrees when we left Perth."

"Try thirty-two degrees here."

As Marc drove the four of them back to the caravan park, he constantly looked in the rear-vision mirrors. He parked the car at the van, and Barney and Helena carried in their two large cases.

Jodie stared. *What on earth's in those cases? And where the heck can they go out of the way?* "I guess you two had better put your gear up the back of the van with the double bed."

Helena waved her hand. "Don't let us put you out."

"You won't." She pointed to the lower bunk at the front of the van. "This is Marc's bunk. I have the double bed to myself."

Helena reddened, and Barney put his hand over his mouth.

Jodie ignored them. "I'm sorry, but I haven't got any spare sheets."

"No problem, I threw some in."

While Jodie took her sheets off the double bed and made up the bunk above Marc's, Helena sorted out her gear and Barney's.

Then they sat down to lunch. Over cups of tea, Marc handed around Jodie's sketch of the Wong brothers and the photos of them.

Barney picked up the photocopy of the photo of Mr. Wong Sr. "I presume this is the patriarch."

Marc gave him the thumbs-up sign. "Spot on."

Helena studied the sketch of the Wongs. "I love this, Jodie. Barney said you were an artist. Have you got any other pieces of your work here?"

Jodie produced the two paintings of the street parade she was working on.

"Wow, take a look at this Chinese dragon, Barney.

He just about jumps out of the painting at you."

Barney looked up from one of the photos on which Jodie had based her painting. "Let's hope Mr. Wong Sr. and the two Mr. Wongs Jr. don't do the same."

After lunch, Marc and Jodie took Barney and Helena on a tour around Broome. Helena fanned herself with a tourist brochure. "Gee, it's hot enough. How do you two cope with the heat?"

As he drove around, Marc constantly checked his rear-vision mirrors. Every time he did it, Jodie's stomach clenched.

****

Helena gave a big yawn. "Lovely chicken salad dinner, thanks, Jodie. Gee, I'll be glad to crawl into bed and flake out tonight. With the lousy hours Barney's been working lately and the rush to organize coming up here, we're quite sleep-deprived. It's lovely to have this chance of a holiday to catch up."

Marc laughed. "Did I hear someone say 'holiday'? You'd better enjoy tonight then because it will be a pretty long day tomorrow and we've got the Mardi Gras in the evening."

****

Over breakfast the following day, Marc looked at Barney and Helena. "You two organized to go off on police business this morning?"

They nodded.

"But, seeing we're going to be on duty at the Mardi Gras tonight, do you reckon we deserve a swim at Cable Beach this afternoon?"

Helena eyes lit up. "Would we what? Why do you think we came?"

While the three detectives were off on police work,

Jodie worked on her paintings. *Lovely to lose myself in the color and texture of my paints and recreate things I love about Broome.*

****

On the way to Cable Beach, Helena and Jodie sat in the back seat. Jodie squirmed around and looked out the back window. "Have you noticed the number of times Marc's checked his rear-vision mirror and Barney's checked his from the front passenger seat? Somehow, I think they're on duty 24/7."

Helena shrugged. "Don't let it get at you—it's what cops do. Even me. But you'll see, we'll still manage to enjoy the holiday."

Jodie nodded. *Lovely to have a friend who understands how I feel about Marc's dangerous work.*

The four of them rushed into the cool water at Cable Beach. Jodie dived in. *How silly, I almost expect Joe to be swimming along with me like a dolphin as he did before.* As she surfaced, it was Marc swimming beside her. He smiled.

Jodie trembled. *Oh, Marc, while we're in Broome, why can't you shave off your beard and return Joe to me?* As Marc struck out into deeper surf, she trembled again. *I know I love you as Marc as well, but it's as if you're quads and I'm in love with you all. First you're the lost boy I fell in love with, then the awakening policeman, then the tough guy cop, and now some funny mix of the three of you. Why can't you let me have you all?*

Helena surfaced from a dive through a wave. "This is glorious."

Jodie grinned. "It's your first time here, isn't it?"

"Yes, but it won't be my last. I've never seen such

a long, white beach."

After half an hour in the surf, Jodie collapsed on her towel alongside the others and closed her eyes. "Want some more sunscreen?" a male voice said. *Joe, I can't believe it.* Her eyes flew open.

Marc's bearded face smiled back at her.

"Great, thanks, Marc." *The warmth of your hand, or maybe Joe's hand, circling my back is burning into me like the hot sun. If you're not careful, I'll purr like a cat.* Minutes later she changed positions with him, and she became the one applying the sunscreen. *It's like the first time I moved my hand over Joe's back.* Her cheeks burned.

Several hours, two swims and two sunbaking sessions later, Jodie sat up and looked around. As though changing position, she lay down again. This time she placed her mouth close to Marc's ear. "Don't look now, but there are two guys up near the car park and they've binoculars pointed down this way."

Marc turned his face toward her. "Are they the Wongs?"

"Very likely. From this distance they look pretty like them—dark, youngish, slim, not terribly tall."

Marc turned his head and passed the word to Barney who passed it to Helena. Then Marc casually sat up and glanced around as though enjoying the scenery. As he turned to face the sea, Barney sat up and did the same. Jodie sat up without looking around, as did Helena.

Jodie rubbed her nose. "Well, what do you guys reckon?"

Marc exhaled audibly. "Couldn't be anyone else but them."

"The thing is, what are they after?"

Barney's face hardened. "If someone's tipped them off I'm here, they'll be wanting a good look at me."

Jodie's face drained of color. "And Helena."

"No, she's unofficial. Not even Masters knows I've sneaked her along in my overnight bag."

"You think Scott Masters is the one who tipped them off?"

"The most likely possibility. What do you reckon, Marc?"

"Yes, or it could have been the guy at the hire-car place, someone at the airport, or even old Gilbert at the caravan park."

Jodie gulped. "Got your guns somewhere?"

Marc looked down at his and Barney's naked torsos. "We've hardly got them on us."

They all laughed.

As the four of them headed up to the car park, the men watching them walked off. Approaching their car, Jodie tilted her head back, and her hat fell off. As she picked it up, she looked around. "They're getting into a car parked two rows behind our car."

Marc took a casual look. "It's definitely the Wong brothers, and we're obviously going to have their company back to Broome. There's not much I can do to shift them around here, but hold on to your hats when we get to town."

In the main shopping center, there was the usual bottleneck of traffic around the car park at the food store. Marc pulled into one side of the car park, did a loop of it, and then accelerated out the far side. Jodie glanced back at the Wong brothers and let out a laugh. "They were trying to follow us but couldn't keep up.

They tried to do a turn and blocked two lanes. Now they've caused a traffic jam and got themselves jammed in on either side."

Barney grinned. "Serves them right. But damned if I know what they hope to get out of following us—we should be following them."

Back at the caravan park, Jodie and the others went off to shower before getting ready for the Mardi Gras.

When Jodie returned from the showers, she walked in on two Spaniards in the van. "My god!"

The woman with long flowing black hair straightened her red peasant blouse and held out her full black skirt with a red trim and curtsied. The man with longish, shiny, black hair in a ponytail wore a white ruffled shirt with long full sleeves and tight, black flared pants. He stamped his feet and clicked his fingers above his head. "Ole!"

Helena's smile wreathed the face of the woman under the long black wig. "I'll just finish my makeup and then you can get dressed up here if you like."

"You both look incredible. If I'd bumped into you outside, I wouldn't have known it was you two."

"That's the idea. Here, put this on, and see what it does for you." She handed Jodie something folded in a plastic bag.

Shortly afterwards a soft tap came at the door. Slowly Marc pushed open the door. "Everyone decent?" He looked around at the trio of two Spaniards in traditional garb and a stunning redheaded beauty. "Wow! I think I must have come to the wrong van."

Jodie gawped at his cleanshaven face. "What have you done, Marc?" Impulsively she pulled the wig of bushy red hair off her head. "See what you look like in

193

this." She threw the wig to him.

As Jodie and Marc put the final touches to their appearances, Helena looked them up and down. "The long-sleeved black tunic top over those long black stretch pants completes your new look, Jodie." She gave her the thumbs up. "Without your beard and with your curly sandy-colored wig covering your dark hair, Marc, you look a different person too." She grinned and gave him the thumbs up as well.

Jodie groaned. *Not another different Marc.* Then she took a closer look at him. *The jungle fatigues you're wearing make you look like an adventurer. You're enough to make any girl's heart skip a beat. You certainly make mine skip. But, despite that sandy wig, you're still my Joe.*

With her face plastered in thick make-up and with the red wig concealing her short blond hair, Jodie assumed a pose. With her hand up to her right ear and her right hip stuck out, she fluttered her eyelashes at Marc. "'Ello, you like?"

Barney gave a low whistle and Helena pulled her camera out of her bag. "Time for photos. We must have some photos."

On the way to the Mardi Gras, Marc dropped Helena and Barney off on the outskirts of town to make their own way in while he and Jodie continued by car. A block away, Marc stopped the car and got out.

Jodie slipped into the driver's seat and drove on to the hire car place. She walked up to the receptionist. "I'm sorry but this car is too big for me to handle comfortably in traffic."

When Jodie drove out, she drove out in a small gray car. *Phew, thank goodness she didn't offer me the first car we hired.* She picked up Marc, and they drove to a large park where he asked her to pull up. Then they walked off in the direction of the music and noisy gaiety of the Mardi Gras.

At an outdoor bar in the center of all the street activity, Helena and Barney sat at an outside table under a palm tree. Jodie coughed. "Don't look now, but there are our friends sitting under the palm tree."

Marc nodded. "I'll buy you a drink." As he walked off, Jodie sat at a nearby table and looked around. A group of young Indigenous people laughed and danced in the street.

Marc returned with a glass of non-alcoholic apple cider and placed it in front of Jodie. "The big guy in the green checked shirt is Ben, Lucas's son. Lucas and some of his mates are farther over. Act as though I've said something funny."

Jodie gave a low laugh and shook her bushy red hair. "You say the funniest things." In a lower voice, she added, "Tell me, is anything expected of me tonight other than to sit here, look beautiful, and laugh at non-existent jokes?" She gave another laugh and picked up her glass.

Marc smiled and raised his glass of cider to her. "The Wongs have set up a deal with the Aborigines tonight. Very soon they'll be passing across a large quantity of heroin to Ben. They think they've talked him into being their pusher to local Aborigines."

Her hand to her mouth, Jodie smothered a laugh. "Gee, you are funny." She took another sip of cider. "Do Barney and Helena know everything that's going on?"

"Yes, I sorted them out this morning."

"I could get offended that you've left it so long to tell me then."

"Sorry, no use weighing you down with police business until absolutely necessary."

Pinning on a flirtatious smile, Jodie flicked back her hair. "Don't ever do that again. I'm not a child, and someone's life might depend on what I know."

"Sorry, I should have known better, Detective."

Jodie fluttered her false eyelashes at him. "Not to worry. I might even forgive you if you ask me to dance."

Marc finished his drink and stood up.

A wicked seductress in her long black top and pants, Jodie stepped into his arms.

"Sexy piece." His eyes scarcely straying from the wider scene around them, he rested his cheek against hers.

"You like my red hair, do you?"

"Gorgeous."

"Like me to wear it all the time?"

Holding her away from him, Marc gave her an exasperated look. "You're my Jodie whatever you look like." He pulled her back to him. "But if you push me for an answer, I do like what I had before just a tad better. Your twin sister is light relief and fun to flirt with, but give me the real thing long term. Okay?"

"Okay." *Maybe now you'll start to see how it is for me with Joe and the three Marcs.*

As Barney and Helena got up to join the swelling throng of dancers, Jodie whispered, "Dancing makes it easier to see what's going on, doesn't it?" She smiled up at Marc and fluttered her false eyelashes at him again.

He laughed and dropped a light kiss on her nose. "You're a knowledgeable little minx, aren't you?"

"Don't get carried away and kiss off all my makeup and give away all my secrets, will you?"

Marc stiffened. "Don't breathe, my sweet—the Wong brothers have just made an entrance."

Jodie giggled. "I love the Marx brothers," she whispered. "They're so funny." *But the chill inside me doesn't match the balmy evening.*

Glancing across at Barney and Helena, Marc nodded imperceptibly. As he spun Jodie around in a dance step, she faced the Wong brothers. "They don't seem a bit interested in you or me. They're too busy looking at some young Aboriginal people dancing in a group. Now they're heading off to the bar."

Marc and Jodie danced on, and he kissed her on the cheek.

Ben left his friends and pushed his way through the dancers to the bar. As he went by, Marc bumped him with his elbow. "Sorry, mate."

Ben glanced up into his face. Marc winked. Although Marc and Jodie continued to dance for another minute or so, they stayed in the same part of the street. Then Marc asked, "Like another drink, gorgeous?"

"Love one, thanks, good-looking." As they made their way over to the bar, Barney and Helena headed there too.

"You and Helena buy the drinks," Marc whispered. He walked into the pub nearby and Barney followed. As she stood next to Helena at the street bar as though they had just met, Jodie gave a laugh. "Men. Always needing to go off to powder their noses."

The girls bought their drinks and carried them to small neighboring tables near the front door of the pub. As they sipped their drinks, there was a sudden movement near them. Ben shot out of the pub, raced into the street, and lost himself among the dancers.

Jodie frowned. "Strange. I wonder what that was all about."

Helena gave a fake laugh. "The boys wanted him out of the way so they didn't have to arrest him."

Jodie took a sip of her drink. After some minutes, she started to shift position and look about. "Why isn't there some follow-up? Why haven't the boys come back?" She forced a smile. "Something's wrong, I can feel it."

"I'm going into the pub to have a look." Helena stood up.

"Have you got a gun?"

Helena nodded. "Mind the drinks."

"No, I'm coming with you."

"No way, Jodie. Give me five minutes. If I'm not back then, go for the local police."

Four minutes later Helena returned. She sat down and gave a light laugh. "It seems our guys have dumped us. There's no sign of them."

Jodie forced a happy expression on her face. "How did you know where to go?"

"Marc arranged with Ben to stick a tiny red sticker on the door of the room the Wongs took him into. I went down the passage and, on the left, a short way from the entrance found Room Thirteen with a sticker on its door. When I burst in, no one was there, and there was no other exit. I tried all the other rooms, and, boy, did I disturb a few people in compromising situations.

But that was it. I'm going to do a trip around the outside of the pub and see what I can find. Stay here in case the guys come back, will you?"

As Jodie sat taking sips of cider, she looked around her. A familiar figure walked by on the far side of the street. *Lucas.*

He stopped to talk to an Indigenous man.

Jodie glanced away and studied the people dancing between her and Lucas. *Should I make my way through the dancers to talk to him?*

Two people were moving through the throng of dancers and coming her way. She froze. *Scott Masters.* He was following a young Chinese man who walked past her table. Jodie held her breath. *Scott Masters is so close I could put out a hand and touch him. But he hasn't recognized me. This Mardi Gras outfit must be some disguise. His mind is obviously on something far more important to him than looking out for me.*

Jodie bit her lip. *What can I do?* Impulsively, she jumped up and followed him and his companion down the passage. As they disappeared into a room on the left, she hurried down to it. *Room Thirteen!* Taking a quick look around, she put her eye to the keyhole. The young man was standing at a fireplace opposite her, and his hand was touching something on the wall beside him. Suddenly, the floor opened and a set of stairs going down into the opening appeared in front of him. He beckoned Scott Masters to follow him down the stairs.

Jodie trembled. *I don't believe it.* Footsteps sounded. *Someone is coming down the passage.* She bent down and fumbled with her shoe.

The barman stopped beside her. "Something

wrong?"

"No, my shoe's giving trouble. Can you tell me where the ladies' room is, please?"

"You've passed it." He gave her a searching look. "It's on the right at the start of the passage."

Taping a smile to her face, Jodie hurried back to the ladies' room. After a suitable time, she emerged, smiled at the barman, who was back behind the bar, and hurried out into the street.

Coming from the other direction, Helena almost bumped into her. Jodie grabbed her hand. "Dance with me."

"I couldn't find anything," whispered Helena.

"I think I know where they are." Jodie gave a light laugh and whispered in her ear.

"That's monstrous! This is way, way too big for us—we need help."

"The car's over on the far side of the park. Start heading off, and I'll catch up with you in a few minutes. First I'll tell Lucas what's going on."

When Jodie got near Lucas and his friend, Jodie pretended to trip and half-fell on him. "Lucas, it's me, Jodie, Joe's girl."

Not showing he had heard anything outrageous, Lucas helped her straighten up. She whispered, "Follow me. We've got to talk."

Under shelter of the darkness of a big leafy tree in a poorly-lit part of the park, Lucas and his friend caught up to Jodie. Helena stepped from behind the tree. Jodie put out her hand. "This is my friend, Helena. Helena, Lucas." The two shook hands.

Lucas touched the arm of the man with him. "This my brother, Monty."

Jodie smiled. "You saw Ben run out of the pub?"

The men nodded. "Well, Marc—you now know that's Joe's real name, don't you?"

Lucas nodded.

"Marc and his policeman friend Barney—Helena's husband—have disappeared. I think I know where they are, but it's too dangerous to look for them without police to back us up. Marc and Barney were supposed to have had back-up from Sergeant Nakamura and his men but there's been no sign of them. Any idea what's happened to them?"

"Sergeant Nakamura a good man. Somet'in' bad musta 'appened to 'im. We better get over to the lock-up and see what we c'n find." Turning to Monty, Lucas fired off instructions in an Indigenous language.

Monty ran off.

Chapter 17

Jodie pulled into the car park at the police station. The station was in darkness. Helena jumped out of the car and ran to the front door. She tried to open it. "Blast!" She rattled it hard.

Lucas ran from his car. "Bang, bang, bang!"

Jodie followed and caught up to him. "Sorry?"

"Someone or somet'in' inside go 'Bang, bang, bang!' You lis'en."

Jodie and Helena listened intently. Bang, bang, bang!

Helena nodded. "You're right, Lucas. The banging's almost continuous now." She took an object out of her handbag and started to poke at a window.

Jodie looked on. "What are you doing?"

"I haven't arrested guys for breaking and entering without picking up a few tips." Helena maneuvered a screwdriver under a catch and grunted as the catch gave. "There." She opened the window. "Bunk me up, will you, guys?"

Jodie reddened and whispered to Lucas, "Helena's a detective."

With their hands, she and Lucas made a step for Helena and she climbed up through the window. Seconds later the door opened.

Helena stood back to let them in. "Don't turn on the light! I've got a torch." She turned it on. The torch beam picked up four bound-and-gagged police officers lying on the floor.

Jodie thumped her forehead with her hand. "My gosh, just look at these guys." Quickly she, Helena, and Lucas rushed over and untied them.

Sergeant Nakamura rubbed his wrists where the rope had bitten into them. "Thanks. Are we glad to see you!"

Helena took out her notebook. "What happened?"

"As we were leaving for the hotel, masked men, presumably sent by Mr. Wong Sr., ambushed us. What happened to the drug bust?"

Helena filled in Sergeant Nakamura and his men. She frowned. "Do you think we should just bowl up to the hotel and charge into Room Thirteen and go down the secret stairway?"

Sergeant Nakamura shook his head. "Not if we want to find Marc and Barney alive."

Jodie grabbed the back of a chair. "But we must do something."

"No, but I know something no one else does." A strange smile played around his lips. "Come on, we've got to get to the Wongs' house. It's across the park from the hotel. On the way I'll tell you a story."

Sergeant Nakamura travelled with Jodie, Helena, and Lucas while the other police followed in a police vehicle. "Thanks to my surname, you might not suspect it, but my paternal grandmother was born a Wong."

Jodie sucked in her breath.

"When she married my grandfather, who was half Japanese, part Aboriginal, and part Malay, she was disowned by her family."

Jodie shook her head. *This story is getting more*

and more fantastic.

"The man you know as Mr. Wong Sr., Mr. Big, is the son of my paternal grandmother's older brother. That makes him my father's cousin. So, our Mr. Wong is actually my first cousin once removed."

Jodie gripped the steering wheel tighter. *Oh, no! Where does that leave us and Marc and Barney?*

Helena asked, "How do you feel about Mr. Wong Sr.?"

"I would like to honor him as my kin, but we have never met socially. When someone treats you as his social and genetic inferior, and worse, as though you don't exist, it is very difficult. Besides it's my job to uphold the law, and I have to do that regardless of what my family connections might be."

Helena nodded. "Any ideas on how to go about rescuing Marc and Barney?"

"Yes. They will probably be being held in the Wong house where we're going now."

Jodie glanced at him. "How do you know?"

"Because when the Japanese became involved in World War Two, and the women and children had to be evacuated, Great-grandfather Wong didn't want that to happen to his wife and children. So he faked their evacuation. He also had a great fortune he didn't want to lose if the Japanese took over Broome. To hide both his family and his fortune, he had a tunnel built from the hotel, which he owned, to his house across the park.

"Various underground rooms were built off the tunnel to hold provisions and bedding and his fortune. Whenever there was danger of an airstrike, the family retreated underground."

Jodie shook her head.

"Though Grandfather Nakamura was only half Japanese, the authorities still wanted to intern him for the duration of the war. But, because he was experienced with earthmoving equipment, Great-grandfather Wong offered to hide him from the authorities if he would work on his tunnel and underground home."

"Incredible."

"That's how my grandmother and grandfather came to meet. Then, once the underground tunnel and home were built, Great-grandfather Wong continued to employ Grandfather Nakamura for general duties. So my grandparents-to-be were able to carry on a secret courtship under his nose."

Again Jodie shook her head.

Helena frowned. "What makes you think Marc and Barney will be in the house and not underground?"

"An educated guess. It would have cost too much to keep the underground in use in any big way."

Jodie gave an involuntary shiver. *I'm not so sure. What better place to dispose of unwanted guests?*

As she drove along the quiet side street alongside the park, Sergeant Nakamura pointed. "Pull up under that wide, leafy tree, thanks." He and Helena got out, and Jodie and Lucas went to follow.

Helena held up her hand. "Sorry, Jodie and Lucas, you guys need to stay here. This is police business."

Jodie clenched and unclenched her fists. *After all we've been through, and now you pull rank on me, Helena.* She watched Helena and Sergeant Nakamura go off.

From the back seat, Lucas reached forward and touched Jodie lightly on the shoulder. "You okay?"

Blinking furiously, she nodded.

"Marc and Barney an' the others be righ', you see."

"I hope you're right, Lucas. I just hope you're right."

"I think it time I got goin' to see where that Monty and Ben got to. You okay if I leave you 'ere and go find 'em and bring 'em 'ere for back-up?"

"Of course."

He stared through the gloom at her white face. "Not they be needed."

Morosely Jodie slumped down low in the car. *No use attracting attention if someone comes along.*

Some time later, she shifted position. *Please,* let *something happen. If the silence and lack of action go on much longer, my head will explode.*

Car headlights swept her car and then headed up the drive to the Wong house. Jodie's scalp prickled, and she peered out at the dark vehicle in the dark drive. *Be careful what you wish for.*

Minutes later, a dark figure jumped up from the ground beside her car door. It thrust a gun through her part-open window. "Get out!"

Jodie froze.

"You heard me!"

She opened the door and got out. The man holding the gun gestured to her to start walking in front of him. *You're the young Chinese man who took Scott Masters into the hotel.* He marched her up the drive to the house, touched something on the front door, and then pushed the door open.

Inside a spacious lounge room, Sergeant Nakamura and three of his officers held an older Chinese man, the two Wong brothers, and a flushed Scott Masters at gunpoint. Helena and two disheveled men covered in dirt stood, guns drawn, on the far side of the room. Jodie's heart leapt. *Marc and Barney, you're safe.*

In the floor next to the men was an opening and, from it, a stairway led down into the depths. Jodie tingled. *The other end of the underground passage.*

The young Chinese man beside Jodie went white. "Anyone move, and this woman gets it!" He rammed his gun against her head. She winced.

Sergeant Nakamura's gun wavered.

Marc took a step forward. "Don't hurt her!"

Jodie's legs buckled. *Whatever you do, Marc, don't throw down your gun. I must do something.* "Nobody move! If you give in to this man, all of us, not just me, will be killed." She took a deep breath. "This man is only bluffing anyway—he's too intelligent to kill me. He knows if he does, he'll be arrested for cold-blooded murder. With so many witnesses, he'll get life imprisonment. But if he surrenders and helps police nobble these drug barons, the courts will go easy on him."

Sweat glistened on Mr. Wong Sr.'s forehead. "Don't take any notice of her, Chan. You will be handsomely rewarded for your loyalty to me."

Marc moved another step closer to Chan and Chan's finger tightened on the trigger. "Chan, you're only small fry to the police. We've got nothing on you—we're after the big guys like Mr. Wong Sr. and Scott Masters here. Unless you commit murder, we've got next to nothing on you. Here, give me your gun." Hand outstretched, Marc walked toward him.

Chan licked his lips. "Stay where you are!"

Mr. Wong Sr. pushed past Sergeant Nakamura,

darted behind Helena and Barney, and then charged down the stairs.

Barney went to follow, but the floor closed up. He whipped his leg away just before it was crushed. He shoved his gun into the side of one of the Wong brothers. "Open it up!"

The brother looked at Chan. The color of a seasick stick of broccoli, Chan was handing his gun to Marc. Marc passed it on to Jodie. With clammy hands, she took it.

Marc grabbed the second Wong brother. "The button, Wong!" But Helena was already pushing a button on the wall and the floor was opening. She and Barney jumped down the stairs and Marc followed.

Sergeant Nakamura gestured to one of his officers. "Handcuff these men and keep them covered until we get back." He jerked his head at two other officers. "You help, and then go to Room Thirteen at the hotel. Find the button to open up the floor like the one does here. Run down the stairs and along the underground passage until you meet Wong Sr. or me coming from this end." Then he too disappeared down the stairs.

Quickly, the policemen handcuffed the Wong brothers, Chan, and Scott Masters. As two officers ran off, Jodie ran after to them to the door. "The button's at shoulder height on the left side of the fireplace."

Gun still in her hand, she turned and walked up to Scott Masters sitting on the couch. Her face etched in disgust, she stared at him. "How could you do it?"

"It's all been a terrible mistake. I've been working as a double agent. I was about to lift the whole lid on this concern, but O'Connors and Baker beat me to it."

Jodie's lip curled. *You loathsome scum.*

"Those two boys are fine young policemen—I'll recommend them for bravery awards and immediate promotion."

Jodie rolled her eyes and looked at the faces of the Chinese men listening in. *To use a stereotype term, which currently couldn't be more appropriate, your faces are inscrutable.*

Twenty minutes later, Marc emerged from the stairwell. A handcuffed Mr. Wong Sr. followed, with Barney holding a gun at his back. A smiling Ben followed them. Jodie's mouth fell open. "Who else have you got down there?"

Helena, Monty, and Lucas followed. Lucas threw her a wink. "Our friends are outside."

Jodie shook her head.

At the police station, Marc, his colleagues, and his friends watched the police vehicle disgorge its prisoners. As police officers led them away, Sergeant Nakamura turned to Marc. "They'll be held safely in the cells for the night. Let's go to my office now for a debriefing."

Once seated in the office, he and the others looked at Marc expectantly. Marc took a deep breath. "Earlier tonight after Barney and I left Helena and Jodie at the street bar, we ran into the pub. Just as the Wong brothers were exchanging a packet of heroin with Ben for a packet of money, we burst into Room Thirteen. We rushed over to them with our guns. As pre-arranged, Ben fled out of the room. But one of the brothers must have pressed a secret button because the floor opened beneath our feet, and we both fell down a flight of stairs. It's a wonder neither of us was killed."

Jodie almost sobbed aloud. *Your head. You could*

have hit your head.

Barney rubbed his left elbow. "You can say that again. When we gathered our wits, the Wongs were standing over us with our own guns. They frog-marched us along an underground passage to a storeroom and threw us in. They tied us up and left us lying on the dirt floor. It was pretty cold and uncomfortable there, so it was really something when we heard Helena running along the passage and calling to us."

Helena put her hand on his arm. "Yes. When Sergeant Nakamura, his men, and I burst into the house, we took the Wongs completely by surprise. But there was no sign of Marc and Barney at all. We guessed they had to be in a secret underground room somewhere. So we looked for a matching button to the one at the pub. As you'd said where you'd seen the matching button in Room Thirteen, Jodie, we soon found it. After that, there wasn't much to it."

Jodie's face tightened. "What did you guys think when you saw Scott Masters with the Wongs?"

Barney snorted. "Helena had already warned us he was in the house, so we made a point of ignoring him."

Jodie pursed her lips. "He told me he was a double agent about to blow the lid on the whole Wong operation."

The others burst out laughing.

Marc scowled. "He'll have to have a top lawyer and good back-up to get to first base with that one!"

Barney nodded. "I hope the louse rots in jail until his case comes to court."

A chill passed through Jodie. "You don't think any of them will get out on bail?"

Sergeant Nakamura sniffed. "Anything's possible, but we'll certainly oppose bail."

Jodie turned to Marc. "Hey, you still haven't told me how you caught up with Mr. Wong Sr."

He nodded in Ben's direction. "Thank Ben for that."

Ben grinned.

Lucas put up two thumbs. "Yes. After I left you, I first found Monty who'd gone off looking for Ben. Then together we found Ben with his friends. When I mentioned the underground tunnel to him, Ben remembered that he'd turned as he was rushing out of Room Thirteen to escape from Marc and Barney. He said he'd got a glimpse of the floor opening. That's why he, Monty, and I decided to investigate that. Meanwhile, we sent Ben's mates to stake out the Wongs' house."

Marc nodded. "After they'd worked out how to get into the underground tunnel, Ben and co were making their way along it when they heard footsteps running toward them. They flattened themselves into an alcove. When Ben peeped out and saw the person running was Mr. Wong Sr., he put out his foot to trip him up. By the time Barney and I arrived, he'd already made a citizen's arrest."

Jodie beamed. "Good for you, Ben."

****

In the shower, Jodie raised her face. *Nothing like warm water to cleanse away all the grime of the day in every sense.* By the time she returned to the van, the others were already in bed. As she went to climb up into her bunk, Marc's hand reached out for her. "Please, Jodie, I need to know you're beside me tonight."

Her knees buckled. *After what we've been through, he needs the comfort of my nearness as much as I need his.* She did not resist as he pulled her into his bunk. Sighing, he wrapped his body around hers and his kiss was as light as a butterfly on her mouth.

In the darkness, she touched his face. "Your beard. Thank you for shaving off your beard. But why?"

"Well, you said you wanted Joe back and I thought maybe it would help me remember him if I made myself as much like him as possible."

"You're a lovely man, do you know that? Maybe I should put that red wig back on so you can have What's-'er-name back?"

"No, you're wonderful just the way you are."

Jodie let herself unwind. *What peace, what bliss.* Stifling a groan of pleasure, she turned her back on Marc and pushed her hips into his groin. Locked in the fetal position, she closed her heavy eyelids and immediately fell sleep. Marc kissed the back of her neck. There was no response. He pulled a face and closed his eyes.

Chapter 18

In the morning, Jodie stirred. Something warm was wrapped around her back. Feeling around it, she reached the back of Marc's waist. *Joe.*

Her eyes flew open. *Hey, Barney and Helena are in here with us.* Her head whirled around. The double bed was empty. "Oh no, they've already seen us." His eyes still shut, Marc turned and followed Jodie's body around. Reaching his hands around her waist, he pulled her hips back into his groin. "No, Marc, we've got to get up."

She threw back the covers, jumped out, and grabbed her clothes. As she started to pull them on, she glanced back and found Marc watching her with a smile on his face. "Turn your head the other way."

As Jodie collected her washbag, Marc pushed back his bedcovers and lazily stood up. When he started to unbutton his pajama buttons, Jodie quickly pushed past saying, "I'm off to the amenities block. See you."

Over breakfast, Marc tapped on his glass. The others stopped talking. "What do you guys want to do after we go to the police station, tie up any loose ends, and get the paperwork out of the way?"

Helena sniffed. "Let's hope our friends haven't found themselves some great lawyer who's already got them out on bail."

Jodie's face tightened, but she said nothing.

Helena got up and started to clear the table. "After we finish at the police station, how about we spend the rest of the day at Cable Beach?"

Marc gave her a high five. "Suits me! Throw your beach gear in the car, and we'll see what we can do."

At the police station, a photographer ushered them in, and Sergeant Nakamura got up from his desk. Marc strode over to him. "What's going on?"

"News leaked out about last night. When the editor of the local paper rang, I told him you'd be here this morning. Hope you don't mind. They want some shots of you fellows by yourself and some with our men."

"Fair go, we were only doing our job."

"Well, your job makes news, and the paper wants to run with the story."

"Have you cleared it with my boss…whoever he is now?"

"Of course."

Pulling a face, Marc allowed himself to be pushed into position with Barney, Helena, Jodie, and the police officers involved in the arrest. "What about Ben, Lucas, and Monty?"

"All taken care of." The door opened and one of his police officers came in with the three men. Grinning widely, they joined in the photo session.

****

Marc and Barney came out of the change room at Cable Beach. Helena threw her hands over her eyes. "Ye gods, look at you! Your backs, arms, and legs are black and blue with bruises."

Marc and Barney posed and showed off their trophies from the night before. In an exaggerated fashion, Barney and Marc hobbled down to the beach.

Like an old man, Marc bent forward and sighed. "Don't expect our usual Olympic swimming performances, will you, ladies?"

After lunch, Helena and Barney went for a walk along the beach, and Jodie set up her easel and paints on the grassed area above Cable Beach. *Oh, Marc, do you have to lie in a Joe-like position on the grass like that? The ache building up for him in me is getting unbearable.*

"What are you thinking?"

"Nothing."

"Hey, it's me—no need to be shy."

Jodie took a deep breath. "How much did you like the redhead you took out last night?" With exquisite concentration, she applied blue paint to the sky on her canvas.

"She was great—a real turn-on. Why?"

"Do you like her as much as me?"

"Why? Is this some sort of trick question?"

"You wanted to know what I was thinking."

Marc nodded and flopped over onto his bruised back. "Oww, I shouldn't have done that! Anyway, go on."

"Tell me what else you liked about the girl with the red hair."

"Well, she had pluck, didn't she? How many girls do you know would do undercover police work for their boyfriends, and how many would keep their cool if some thug pointed a gun to their head and threatened to shoot?"

"Would you like me to be more like her?"

"What sort of a question is that?" Marc pulled himself onto his feet and went to stand beside her. "She is you—she's just another side of your personality, isn't she?" He leaned across and kissed her lips.

"Marc…" Jodie turned to him, her gaze steadily holding his.

"Yes?"

"Has it ever occurred to you that's the same way I…?"

"…feel about Joe?" He kissed her again. "I know. I've been a jealous old whatever. But how would you like it if I told you I wanted you to wear that ridiculous wig all the time?"

Jodie smiled.

"And to get about all in black? Is that you, the real you?"

Jodie shook her head.

"Well, that's how I feel about Joe. He was such a paragon and…and sometimes you seem to love him more than you love me. And…and…well, damn it, he seemed such a wimp at times. And that's not me at all."

Jodie hid a smile. "No, it's not you, is it? You haven't got a sensitive, lost little boy side to you, have you?"

Marc pulled a face.

"As far as that mad redhead and I go though, I hardly look like her. At least you and Joe look much the same."

Marc rubbed his cleanshaven face. "Now I've taken my beard off, you mean. But I do wear different clothes from Joe."

A gleam in her eyes, Jodie stared meaningfully at his bare tanned chest. "Not now, you don't."

"Okay, truce on Joe and truce on the redhead—you can fantasize about him if I can fantasize about her."

"Oh, you admit it, you do fantasize about her, do you?" Jodie gave him a mock hit with her paintbrush.

"I couldn't help it if she leapt into my bunk last night and started to ravish me." He jumped sideways and averted another hit with the paintbrush.

Jodie glared. "You're hopeless, you know that?"

Marc grabbed her and kissed her until she thumped on his arm.

Pink-cheeked, she sat down on her stool. "If I don't get these paintings finished, Kenny's not going to want to foot the bill for the trip up here, you know." Her prim, schoolmarm voice matched her prim, schoolmarm expression.

On their return to the caravan village, Barney tapped on Marc's arm. "Drop us off at the shop, will you?"

When he and Helena caught up with them in the van afterwards, Barney was waving a key. "Hope you guys don't mind but old Gilbert has managed to find us a spare cabin for the next few nights."

Jodie colored. "But you're welcome to stay here." *I hope you're not shifting because of what you saw this morning and thought you were invading our privacy.*

Barney pulled Helena to his side. "We know, but...we thought we'd take advantage of the chance for a second honeymoon." Putting her arms sideways around his waist, Helena hugged him.

That night, Jodie returned from her shower to an empty van and climbed into the double bed. *Sorry Barney and Helena aren't here, but it is nice to have the van to ourselves again.*

A few minutes later Marc came in and hung up his towel on their makeshift clothesline above the sink.

"Okay if I come down and have a talk with you?" He walked down to Jodie's end of the van. Before she could answer, he pulled back the bedcovers and hopped in.

Her insides went haywire. "I don't think this is a good idea."

"Want to know what I think?" He pulled her full-length against him, and she felt quite faint.

"What?"

"We've got pretty serious, haven't we?"

"I...I don't know."

"What, you've had five hundred other guys lying in bed like this with you, have you?"

"Don't be crude." Jodie pushed him away.

"Sorry, but you're not making this easy for me."

In the semi-darkness of the van, Jodie stared hard at his face. "Go on."

"Well...you know how I feel about you."

Jodie didn't answer.

"You know I love you."

"Sort of."

"Well, I'm saying it now—in capital letters—I LOVE YOU." He kissed the tip of her nose.

"I love you too."

He pulled her close and nuzzled her neck. "Damn it, I didn't plan to say this until I got my full memory back, but I can't wait any longer. Will you marry me, Jodie?"

"Oh, J...Marc," Jodie whispered huskily.

"Yes, you can have Joe too, but only if you accept that he's part of me and not me who's part of him—I can't cope with him otherwise."

"You are wonderful." Her body warm and

welcoming, she pressed herself even closer to him. "Of course I'll marry you."

"Now I've gone over Joe's old stamping grounds, I feel as though I know him even if I've never met the guy."

Jodie kissed Marc soundly.

"But remember, if you have Joe, I get to have that redheaded What's-'er-name as well."

"It's a deal."

Marc's kiss was as gentle as light rain.

Jodie's heart fluttered. *I feel as though I'm in the middle of a rainbow.*

Marc's hands caressed her side and she trembled. Gripping his shoulders, she dug her fingers in. When he moved into position above her, alarm bells went off in her brain. "No, Marc." She turned her lips away from his kiss. "Not yet."

His body pulsated against hers. "You're sending me crazy. Hasn't an engaged person any rights at all?"

"Oh, Marc, I really do want to wait until our wedding night, but, even if I didn't, we haven't taken any precautions."

"Let me love you other ways then." Her neck burned at his kiss, and then his kisses made their way down her neck and into the top of her nightgown.

"Don't. You make it too hard for me."

Raising himself above her and lowering himself down gently onto her, he started to move rhythmically, his body hot and passionate against her own. Some moments later Marc reached a climax and lay exhausted on her damp nightgown. "Oh, Jodie, when did you say our wedding day was going to be?"

****

Light coming into the van woke Jodie. She opened her eyes. "Oh my god!"

Marc stirred. "What's up?"

"There's a man in my bed."

"Go back to sleep—it's only me and I'm harmless." He pulled her backwards into his groin.

"Stop that. It's getting so I won't be able to resist you much longer."

"Good, that's what I like to hear."

"You're impossible." She threw off the bedcovers and rushed for her clothes.

"You could have given an engaged person a kiss before you went."

As Jodie quickly got dressed, he lay on his back with his arms under his head and studied the ceiling.

"How's this then, engaged person?" Jodie bent down and lightly kissed his lips. He grabbed her around the shoulders and pulled her down onto him and kissed her thoroughly.

Meeting up with Barney and Helena for breakfast, Jodie and Marc swapped plans with them for the day.

The four drove to Chinatown together and split into pairs, agreeing to meet an hour later. Marc tucked Jodie's hand inside his arm. "That should give us time to find the engagement ring we want."

Jodie glanced around. "I hope this shop isn't owned by Mr. Wong Sr."

"No chance—I said so."

They browsed along a counter looking at rings with glossy pearls set in gold and platinum settings. Jodie stopped and peered closely at a small pearl in a platinum setting. "This one is just perfect. What do you think?"

"Looks pretty good to me." He nodded to the shop assistant. "Could we try this one, please?"

****

The four friends spent the rest of the morning swimming at Cable Beach. In the afternoon, Barney and Helena went for a drive to see some of the sights while Jodie worked on her paintings for Kenny. She stepped back to look at one of the outdoor theatre. "Not much of an afternoon for you. You could have gone off with Barney and Helena, you know."

"What, and miss out on having my very own engaged person to myself for the afternoon? Not likely."

After Barney and Helena returned from their drive, the four of them had another swim.

On the trip back to Broome, Helena turned to look at the back-seat passengers. "When we get back to the caravan park, you've got to get dressed up to the nines and then be our passengers again. If you haven't got any evening wear, you can wear what you wore to the Mardi Gras, Jodie."

"Why, where are we going?"

"Surprise."

"But we're supposed to be going to the fireworks display tonight."

"All under control."

Their backs to each other, Marc and Jodie dressed for the evening. Marc gave a cough. "Okay, if I turn around now?"

"All clear." Before him stood Jodie in a simple midnight-blue dress.

"Wow. I don't know how to put it, but that color somehow goes with your blonde hair and tan."

"You don't look too bad yourself, engaged person."

The dark-haired man in the neat casual shirt and black pants standing in front of her grinned.

"Very presentable, in fact."

Barney drove to an expensive-looking restaurant overlooking Roebuck Bay. "Okay, everybody out."

Jodie gasped. "What, we're going in here?"

"Yes, it's our engagement present to you. Happy engagement!"

Barney helped Jodie out of the car and gave her a peck on the cheek.

As the two couples sat on the balcony enjoying a tropical salad, there was a sudden staccato outburst. Jodie jumped and went to dive under the table.

Barney laughed. "Take it easy, Jodie. It's only fireworks. It's the start of the fireworks display to mark the end of the Shinju Matsuri festival."

The sky exploded in blazes of lights and colors. Rockets soared skyward and great spluttering fiery circles whirled around in front of them.

Jodie clapped her hands. "Wow! What a sight."

Later she danced cheek to check with Marc. "When have I ever been so happy?"

"I can think of a few times. Like me to make an announcement about them?"

****

As they walked back to the rental car, someone came up behind them and thumped Marc lightly on the shoulder. "Hey, Marc!"

Marc whirled around. "Ben! How's it going?" He and Barney shook Ben's hand, and Helena and Jodie said hello.

"Fine. You know those papers about joining the police force you got me to fill in?"

Marc nodded. "Did you put me down as a referee like I said to?"

"Yeah, and when I took the papers in to get Sergeant Nakamura to check them over for me, he said he'd write me a reference as well."

"What do you know. See what happens when you go around impressing people."

Barney grinned. "Don't forget there's another police officer right here who'll give you a reference too. You helped us all out of a rough spot, remember."

Helena laughed. "How many references do you need, Ben? I can vouch for you, if necessary."

****

By the time she got to bed, Jodie was struggling to keep her eyes open. Marc got back from his shower and climbed into bed beside her. "Are you awake?"

She said nothing and he pulled a face.

****

Light streaming into the van woke Jodie the following morning. Beside her, Marc stirred and reached for her.

"Oh, Marc, I don't think I can handle being with you like this anymore."

"Good." He nipped her ear. "It's about time you admitted this thing is for real."

"What thing?" With a laugh, he pushed himself hard against her.

"Gee, I'll be glad to get back to Perth," she whispered weakly against his mouth.

"Why, don't you like being with me like this?"

"Of course, I do, but I've worked out I'm an all or

nothing person. I can't cope with this being together, not being together thing—I like being with you all the time or at least being with you every night."

"I thought we already had that in hand." He kissed her eyelids.

"You know what I mean." Jodie tried to push him away but he was already turning her onto her back. Raising himself on top of her, he pressed his lips down onto hers and started a long, deep kiss.

Suddenly, there was loud knocking on the door of their van. Jodie pushed at Marc's chest. "My gosh, it must be Helena and Barney." She tried to squirm out from under Marc. "Won't be a minute!"

"Get lost, Barney!" Marc called.

"Ssh, they'll hear you."

"That's the general idea." He rolled off her onto his back and pulled his pillow over his head. "There's no justice in this world."

Jodie partly opened the door and put her head around it.

Helena stood waiting outside. "We thought you guys were never getting up."

Jodie glanced back at Marc with the pillow over his head and laughed. "Well, I don't know about Marc."

"We just want the key to the car so we can pack our gear in it."

After Helena had gone, Jodie went back to Marc and sat beside him on the bunk and placed her hands on his shoulders. "I love you."

"I love you too." He pulled her face down to his and kissed her lightly. "But we're never going to consummate our engagement at this rate."

She gave a giggle. "Who said we were supposed

to?"

"Well, someone's interested here."

"Perhaps it will give us something interesting to do on our wedding night."

A tap came on the door and Helena poked her head inside the van. "You can have the key back now."

"You can come in." Jodie walked up to her.

"Thanks, but we're off for a walk—we haven't had a good look around the caravan park yet."

With a broad grin on his face, Barney pushed in beside Helena and stood looking down the van.

Helena smiled. "Keep an eye on the time, won't you? We have to head off for the plane soon."

Barney laughed out loud, and his wife pulled an exasperated face, grabbed his hand, and dragged him off.

Jodie shut the door behind them and looked back at Marc. He was three-quarters dressed and had a fed-up expression on his face. She grinned. "Oh, come on, it's not that bad."

****

As the plane taxied along the runway and then lifted off, Jodie blinked hard several times. Holding onto her hand, Marc whispered, "Happy?"

"Yes, but I feel as though I'm leaving part of myself behind in Broome."

"I know what you mean. I think I was more Joe here than I could ever be in Perth." He raised their intertwined hands and kissed her fingertips.

Chapter 19

As they stepped into the lounge area at Perth Airport, Jodie and Marc smiled as a small blond girl and a slightly bigger olive-skinned boy with Mediterranean looks ran to throw their arms around Helena and Barney. A middle-aged woman stood watching them.

Jodie studied her. "An older version of Helena."

"Yes, and we'll be Barney and Helena in six or seven years' time."

Jodie blushed. From the back of the waiting crowd at the exit gate, her father waved. "Dad!" She ran and hugged him and her mother next to him and then turned to Tiffany and Ryan. "Gosh, what a welcome-home reception."

Eve hurried over and threw her arms around Marc. "Marc!"

Marc hugged her and turned to the man behind her and extended his right hand to him. "Ian, great to see you again. Thanks for driving Mum in."

Then Jodie kissed Eve. *How happy you look. How much is it to do with you having your son back again and how much to do with having a loving man beside you to share his homecoming?*

Tiffany shoved a newspaper in front of Marc and Jodie. "Have you seen this?"

Marc groaned. "Oh no, they've splashed it all over

the Perth papers as well."

Jodie jabbed at the newspaper Tiffany held up. "These are some of the photos the Broome newspaper reporter took in Broome."

Ryan grinned. "Now you know why we've all come to see you—to rub shoulders with the celebrities."

During dinner at the Winters', Marc tapped his water glass. "Time for official announcements, people."

All looked up, and Jodie leaned her leg against Marc's under the table.

Marc put his arm around her shoulder. "Jodie and I are engaged to be married."

Her face wreathed in smiles, Eve jumped up from the table and kissed Marc and then Jodie. "I'm so pleased for you both."

"The three of us actually, Mum. It's going to be a pretty strange marriage because Jodie would only agree if Joe were part of the mix."

Everyone laughed.

Tiffany waved her hand. "It was only a matter of time. I could see it written all over them ever since they first laid eyes on each other."

Jodie smiled. *Correction—only ever since you took your eyes off Joe, alias Marc, and laid them on Ryan.*

****

The next day Jodie drove out to Marc's for lunch. As they sat around afterwards, Eve asked, "Have you two set a wedding date yet?"

Jodie grinned at Marc. "Not yet."

Marc gave her a wink. "But sooner rather than later. Like tomorrow."

Eve waggled her finger at her son. "What sort of wedding are you having? Traditional?"

He nodded. "We were thinking…"

Jodie glanced out the front window. Over the road, Linda was working in her garden. "Sorry to interrupt, Marc, but you know how we were only going to have a small wedding with Tiffany for bridesmaid and Barney for best man, well, how about…?" She excused herself from Eve and went and whispered in Marc's ear.

He groaned and she punched him lightly on his good arm.

His face broke into a smile and he nodded. "Okay, let's get it over with then." He jumped up. "Watch this, Mum." He and Jodie went out the front door and headed over the road.

At their approach, Linda straightened up from her weeding and, unsmiling, stood up. Marc cleared his throat. "Hi, Linda. We wanted you to be one of the first to know, Jodie and I are engaged to be married."

Her face tightened. "Congratulations. I hope you both will be very happy."

Jodie extended her hand and showed Linda her engagement ring.

"What a dear little ring."

Marc pushed the hair back from his forehead. "Linda, Jodie's sister Tiffany is going to be chief bridesmaid and, because you're the closest thing I've got to a kid sister, we'd like to ask you a favor. Would you be our bridesmaid too?"

As if hit with a pillow in a pillow fight, Linda stood dazed for a few seconds. "Oh, Marc!" She threw her arms around his neck and hugged him. Then she turned and hugged Jodie a little less exuberantly. "That would be wonderful. I really would love that—I've never been a bridesmaid before."

Jodie smiled. "We're asking my brother Kieran to be groomsman so he'll partner you. I'll get Tiff to give you a ring soon to discuss dresses with you."

"Maybe Eve and I could make them and…"

As Marc and Jodie walked back to Eve's, he dropped a kiss on her nose. "Have I ever told you what a lovely generous person you are, engaged person?"

A word about the author...

Meryl Brown Tobin is an Australian writer who writes long and short fiction, non-fiction, poems, and puzzles for adults, teenagers, and children. *Broome Enigma* is her nineteenth published book and first published novel, and there are more in the pipeline. Hundreds of her shorter works have appeared in more than one hundred fifty print and digital publications. Details: http://sites.google.com/site/merylbrowntobin/.

Thank you for purchasing
this publication of The Wild Rose Press, Inc.

For questions or more information
contact us at
info@thewildrosepress.com.

The Wild Rose Press, Inc.
www.thewildrosepress.com